# CHAPTER

## One

THE colorful gourmet jelly beans were lined up across Amanda Roberts's desk in a precise row—lime, grape, orange, ice-blue mint, peanut butter, strawberry daiquiri, banana, chocolate. She studied the orderly procession listlessly, then dug into the jar on her desk for another handful, absentmindedly popping one into her mouth. Licorice, she realized with a grimace. It figured.

"Amanda, you are pathetic," editor Oscar Cates suddenly yelled from halfway across the *Inside Atlanta* office. "Get your lazy butt over here."

"Thank you for your supportive observation," she muttered as she crossed the magazine's newsroom. It was midday and the place was empty. Everyone else was on assignment or out to lunch. Amanda hadn't had any enthusiasm for either. She had barely mustered up

1

sufficient energy to utter one of the verbal barbs that normally highlighted her relationship with her boss. It had been a relatively weak one at that, but Oscar seemed willing to play the usual game.

"I heard that," he muttered right back, then waited expectantly for further, stronger retaliation. When she said nothing, he shook his head in disgust. At the doorway to his office, he gestured her inside. "Get in here and sit down." He observed her dragging gait for about ten seconds, then snapped, "Now, Amanda. Not next week."

Despite the urgency implied by his brusque tone, she noticed that Oscar took his own sweet time settling into the chair behind his desk. He smoothed his few remaining strands of hair. He peered at her over the new reading glasses perched on the end of his nose, then yanked them off in exasperation. He hated those glasses and everything they represented about aging even more than he chafed at the balding. He also hated these little heart-to-heart talks he occasionally found himself obliged to have with employees. No, scratch that. Not *employees*. Mostly with her. Everyone else jumped to do his bidding.

"How much longer is this going to go on?" he asked finally.

"How much longer is *what* going to go on?" she replied vaguely, wondering how many years it would be before working at a computer all day combined with age to make her eyesight start to go just like Oscar's. The dismal prospect suddenly seemed just around the corner. She regarded Oscar bleakly. "I don't know what you're talking about."

"Then you're not half the reporter you're always telling me you are. You've been in a funk ever since you called off the wedding with Donelli."

## Also by Sherryl Woods

*Reckless*
*Body and Soul*
*Stolen Moments*
*Ties That Bind*

# Bank On It

## Sherryl Woods

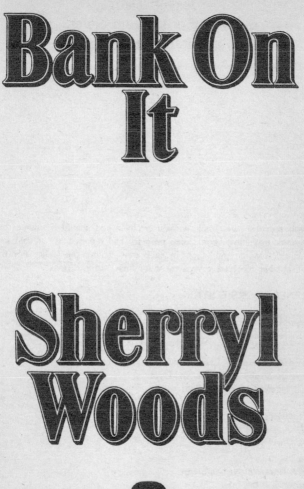

WARNER BOOKS

A Time Warner Company

For Jeanne Tiedge,
every author's dream editor,
with admiration and thanks!

WARNER BOOKS EDITION

Copyright © 1993 by Sherryl Woods
All rights reserved.

Cover illustration by Larry Elmore
Cover design by Jackie Merri Meyer
Hand lettering by David Gatti

Warner Books, Inc.
1271 Avenue of the Americas
New York, NY 10020

W A Time Warner Company

Printed in the United States of America

First Printing: May, 1993

10 9 8 7 6 5 4 3 2 1

It was a low blow, though accurate. She tried to muster up a little indignation anyway. "Excuse me, but I was at the church. He wasn't."

"For good reason."

"I do not consider using me as a pawn in an FBI case justifiable under any conditions."

"Amanda, the man cracked a major case and we got a helluva story," Oscar reminded her. "An exclusive, I might add." He waved his cigar at her for emphasis. In unusual deference to her, he'd left it unlit.

"No, Oscar," she replied patiently. "I cracked the case, by turning half of Georgia upside down to save my missing fiancé, who, as it turns out, wasn't missing at all. And I would have gotten the damned story anyway, if somebody had just bothered to tell me what the hell was going on."

When she realized her voice was climbing, she swallowed hard, then added quietly, "I do not want to talk about this. Joe and I have discussed his questionable tactics until the mere mention of the sneaky, conniving FBI makes me want to throw up. With that warning in mind, pursue the subject at your own risk."

She supposed it was too much to hope that Oscar would actually give up.

He scowled at her. "Amanda, why the hell can't you just forgive the man and get on with the damned wedding? It's over. It's done. Let it go. It's just foolish pride standing in the way."

His was an all-too-typical male reaction. Even Larry Carter, the magazine's primary freelance photographer and one of her very best friends in Atlanta, had suggested the same thing. "If Donelli wasn't your poker buddy and your best pal, you'd know the answer to that," she told Oscar. She'd said the same thing to Larry. The two men had shared the same blank look. They definitely didn't get it.

"I'm not thinking about Donelli," Oscar retorted. "I'm thinking about you. Look at you. You're a mess. You're playing with jelly beans, for God's sake. There hasn't been a sign of the famed Amanda Roberts spunk in weeks. You don't even argue with me, which used to be your favorite pastime. When was the last time you went out of here on an assignment? When was the last time you wrote anything on that computer in there? Do you think we're paying you to sit around here and sulk? The publisher of this magazine is going to start asking questions soon and I don't have any answers for him."

She regarded him without enthusiasm. "So, fire me."

Oscar looked as if she'd asked him to burn down Atlanta for the second time in its history. "Don't even joke like that," he said.

She shrugged indifferently, even though it was the closest Oscar had ever come to giving her a compliment. "I wasn't joking. Maybe that's what I need, a little jolt of reality. Maybe then I'd have the gumption to get out of this godforsaken hellhole and do something with my life."

Oscar rose to his feet at that, practically quivering with Southern indignation. "Young lady, Atlanta is not a godforsaken hellhole. You would never have said anything like that while you were with Donelli."

"Because the man temporarily blinded me to the place's flaws. Apparently he blinded me to a few other things as well, like his macho moralistic code that says the means justify the end, especially if a little flag-waving is involved." She caught her boss's increasingly outraged expression and cut the tirade short. "Never mind. I shouldn't put the burden for this decision on you. I quit."

The words were out of her mouth before she'd had time to think them through, but they'd sounded right, more like a beginning than an end. She could pack her things, put the house on the market, and be back in New York where she belonged by the end of the week. Lord knows what she'd do for a job in the tight journalism market, but at least she'd be home. New York, where creeps mugged their victims straight out, instead of blindsiding them the way Donelli had her.

She stood up and headed for the door, only to find Oscar solidly blocking her path. It was the fastest he'd moved since his wife had allowed him near a buffet table in the middle of his last diet. With his stubbornness combined with his girth, he provided a formidable obstacle.

"Not so fast, young lady," he said.

She backed up a step and held up a warning hand. "Don't try to talk me out of this."

"I wouldn't dream of it. You want to quit, quit. Just know that you'll be walking away from that dream investigative story you've been chomping at the bit to find ever since I've known you. The one that'll get you that Pulitzer Prize you missed out on in New York."

He opened the door then, and stood aside. Because she was too stubborn to do otherwise, Amanda strode right past him. She was actually ten feet away before she stopped and asked in what she hoped was a suitably nonchalant tone, "What story?"

"Nefarious deeds," he said equally casually. Then, as if he were selecting matching pearls and slowly stringing them on a fragile silken thread, he added,

"Banking. Foreign governments. Illegal arms. Let me know when I've caught your interest."

"Here?" she said doubtfully. "In Atlanta?"

"So they say."

"I suppose there are federal investigators all over this, just like last time with that Italian bank?"

"Maybe. Maybe not."

The nonchalant tone and the lure of being one step ahead of the feds suckered her in. She sighed and capitulated. "I'll stay. For a while."

A satisfied smile flitted across Oscar's round face and was gone before she could develop a violent desire to strangle him. She marched back into his office, grabbed a notebook and pen from his desk, and looked up expectantly. There was an undeniable flurry of excitement in the pit of her stomach as she demanded, "Details?"

As she waited for Oscar to cough up information, it occurred to her that the only thing that could top this fever pitch of journalistic anticipation was great sex. With Donelli. *Oh, no,* she warned herself. Definitely a bad train of thought.

"You want details you'll have to go to our source," Oscar said.

"Who is?"

The confident editor squirmed uncomfortably. He rolled down his sleeves and buttoned the cuffs. He hunted for his glasses and put them back on. He shuffled a few papers from one side of his desk to the other without looking at them. At no time did he meet her gaze. It was not the reassuring behavior of a man certain of his information. If it had been anyone else, she might have wondered if he'd made the whole thing up just as she'd headed for the door.

"Oscar, who's the source?" she prodded.

"I'm not exactly sure."

"Excuse me?"

"The guy called about an hour ago."

"Did he have a name?"

He scowled at her. "Of course he had a name, Amanda. He just didn't tell me."

"What exactly did this exceptionally shy source have to say?"

"He asked if we'd be interested in breaking the story of the year. Naturally, I thought of you and said yes."

"Let me get this straight. I am staking my career—to say nothing of my sanity—on an unnamed source who may or may not have information that we can publish about a story that may or may not be true."

Oscar beamed at her quick grasp of the situation. "That's about it. Challenging, huh?"

"Oscar, it really isn't wise to play this kind of game with a woman in my state of mind. I don't have a lot to lose, and murder is beginning to hold an increasing allure. You're rapidly moving past Donelli on the list of prime candidates."

He held out a slip of paper. "Save the threats until after you meet with the guy. If it doesn't pan out, you can hold me up for a bonus or something."

"I will," she said as she glanced at Oscar's nearly illegible scrawl. When she recognized the address, she chuckled despite her sour mood. "You can't be serious. Isn't it a little melodramatic to meet this guy in a cemetery at midnight?"

"I didn't pick the place, Amanda. It was his call."

"I don't suppose you plan to be lurking in the bushes?"

He regarded her innocently. "Would I do that?"

"In a heartbeat. And if not you, you'd send in Larry or Donelli."

"Not this time," he said piously. "You're on your own."

It was an unfortunate choice of words, given her marital circumstances. "So what else is new?" Amanda mumbled as she left Oscar to gloat about his success in rescuing her from her doldrums. For all she knew she'd been right earlier when she suspected he'd invented the whole outrageous damn story for just that purpose. She'd know for sure at midnight. Then, with a clear conscience, she could strangle him for tricking her.

Despite her doubts about Oscar's tale of intrigue, at midnight Amanda dutifully, if not enthusiastically, wound her way through a fog-shrouded cemetery. Eternal Peace Garden of Souls. It was aptly named. The ghostly quiet hung over the place like a shroud. Ancient trees, stripped of their leaves by an early frost and twisted in grotesque shapes, added to the eerie atmosphere. A little Spanish moss swayed in the shadows. If the entire Addams family had stepped out from behind the gravestones and danced a macabre jig, she wouldn't have been the least bit surprised.

Following the instructions Oscar claimed to have been given, she drove to the top of a hill far from the main road and parked her car. The mournful call of an owl sent a shiver down her spine as she used her flashlight to pick out the designated meeting place a hundred feet away.

Just as described, the Howell family vault loomed ahead of her, graced by an angel on top and twin cherubs on either side of the main entrance. Wilted chrysanthemums, mostly brown now, gave the vault an air of neglect. Apparently the recent generation of

Howells didn't waste a lot of time paying homage to their ancestors. It looked as if they'd passed this way around Thanksgiving . . . last year.

Amanda slowly circled the vault, then scanned as much of the graveyard as she could see in the fog. There was no sign of a living creature. She leaned against a cherub to wait, fingering the tape recorder in her pocket for comfort. If no one showed up, at least she could record a new resignation and mail it in to Oscar on her way back to New York, a city she never should have left in the first place.

That familiar sense of desolation returned, stronger now than it had been even after she'd been abandoned a few years back by her husband within weeks after they'd arrived in Georgia. Mack Roberts's betrayal with another woman—a college sophomore, to top it off—had infuriated her. Donelli's betrayal had cut deeper. He had won her trust on every level, overcoming all the barriers she'd put into place after Mack. Then he had abused that trust. She still loved him, God help her, but she doubted she could ever forgive him.

A faint rustling pushed thoughts of the traitorous Donelli from her mind.

"Ms. Roberts?" The male voice floated mysteriously through the fog. He sounded young and anxious. The latter wasn't surprising given their location and the information he claimed to be prepared to impart.

"Yes," she said. "Where are you?"

"Never mind. You don't need to see me. You just need to hear what I have to say."

"I can't go off on some half-cocked investigation unless I know my source is credible."

"That's not what I hear," he said with a touch of

wry humor. "Why do you think I chose you instead of someone on the Atlanta papers?"

"I wasn't aware that you'd chosen me. You called my boss."

"I called you. The receptionist said you weren't taking calls."

Amanda rolled her eyes. In a genuine act of friendship meant to save Amanda's professional hide, Jenny Lee Macon hadn't put a call through to her directly since the day Amanda had told a major advertiser to cancel his ads if he didn't like her attitude.

"So here we are," she said. "What's the story?"

"There's a trade embargo with Iraq, right? We're practically at war with them again."

"Yes."

"What if I were to tell you that a foreign government is using an Atlanta branch of its national bank to see that Iraq gets whatever arms it needs?"

"Old news. That case has already been through the courts."

"No, not the Italians," he said with a trace of impatience. "This is a new scam, new bank."

"I'd say I need proof," Amanda said, her blood beginning to race at the hint of a story that could make international headlines. "What bank? What country? Who's on the inside? I'd need to be able to follow the paper trail from beginning to end. Can you do that for me?"

"Yes," he said. "I work there. I got suspicious about some transactions a few months ago. I've been collecting evidence ever since. I don't have all the pieces, but I think I have more than enough to blow the lid off."

"Do you have it with you?"

"I brought enough to prove—"

There was a quiet pop, no louder than a child's cap pistol muffled by a pillow, but it was effective enough to cut him off in midsentence. Her heart thudding, Amanda heard a dull thump, then nothing.

"Oh, shit," she muttered, her back pressed against the vault as she realized what had happened. One of these days she really was going to have to start carrying that gun she kept at home in the kitchen drawer. Or was it in the closet now? She kept moving it, to her current regret. She couldn't very well dart after the killer with her tape recorder. What would she do? Try to scare him to death by requesting an interview?

For what seemed an eternity she waited for some other sound, but there was nothing, not even the rustling movement of a departing assassin.

When she finally decided it was safe, she crept around the edge of the vault in the direction from which her unidentified source had been speaking. She swung the beam of her flashlight in a slow arc over the ground. She'd covered no more than ten yards when she saw the shadowy form slumped backward over a tombstone, arms akimbo, head thrown back at an awkward angle.

Although she knew it was useless, she felt for a pulse. Nothing. Finally, she looked at him more closely.

He was young. No more than twenty-five or thirty, she guessed with a twinge of regret. There was a look of surprise on his face. He was dressed in jeans, a polo shirt, a linen blazer, and sneakers—a yuppie uniform that provided no clues to his identity. Overcoming her distaste for the task, she patted his pockets in search of a wallet. Either he'd left it behind or the killer had stripped it from him before she'd left her hiding place fifty yards away. There were no car keys that might lead her to an abandoned vehicle in the vicinity. If he had carried any evidence to support his claim, that too was missing. He was, however, still wearing an expensive watch, proving that the motive for the murder hadn't been robbery.

So, she thought wearily, there were no answers for her here, only confirmation that he had indeed had a story to tell and had paid the highest possible price for the attempt to tell it.

Solidly hooked, she was already mapping her investigative strategy as she walked back to her car and picked up her cellular phone to call the police. She would wait there for a police ID of the victim, then try to find out at which bank her would-be source had worked. Maybe she could even think of some way to infiltrate the bank. Obviously, as of now, they had an opening. Unfortunately, what she knew about banking could fit on the tip of a ballpoint pen. She balanced her checkbook with the help of a calculator and several glasses of wine. She doubted any bank would let her drink on the job. Maybe a savings and loan. If recent federal takeovers were any indication, their personnel standards, at least for executives, had to be pretty low.

"Homicide, please," she told the police operator who answered. "Detective Harrison. If he's not in, beep him. It's urgent."

She waited for Jim Harrison to get on the line. She hadn't a qualm in the world about calling him at this hour. He thrived on long hours and complicated cases. He'd love this one. If he felt he owed her for pulling him in from the outset, so much the better. She wanted to be the first person told when the police identified the guy.

"Harrison," the detective grumbled wearily. "Roberts,

what the hell are you doing calling me at one in the morning? Don't tell me somebody finally tagged you for speeding."

"Actually, I'm in a cemetery with a dead body."

"Very funny."

"It might be, except this guy walked in very much alive."

She heard him suck in his breath.

"Details," he said in the same precise, alert tone she'd used earlier with Oscar. She could practically see him reaching for his ever-present pad and pen.

After she'd described the location, he said, "Sit tight. I'll be there in twenty minutes."

"Thanks."

"Stay in your car, Amanda. Don't go frisking the body for clues."

"I wouldn't dream of it," she said piously, thankful it wasn't a lie. She'd definitely done all the frisking she intended to.

It took less than fifteen minutes before she saw a parade of headlights weaving into the cemetery. She figured Harrison had waited until he turned in at the gate before calling in the rest of the troops.

As soon as he stepped out of his car, Amanda opened her own door and walked toward him, noting that his jacket was rumpled as usual. She wondered if they came back from the cleaners that way or if he had a supply like that tangled together in his trunk.

He glanced around at the setting, his expression rueful. "We really must stop meeting like this."

"Oh, I don't know. Whenever I stumble across a murder, I just naturally think of you."

"Are you so sure it's a murder? Maybe the guy had a heart attack sneaking around to meet you in the middle of the night. I can see where keeping up with you might do that to a man.''

''Judge for yourself,'' she said, leading the way toward the body. With Jim Harrison at her side, she circled the Howell vault and headed toward the place she'd last seen her mysterious source.

Unfortunately for her credibility, the only thing draped over the nineteenth-century tombstone now was a coating of moss.

# CHAPTER

## *Two*

"**B**URIED already?" Jim Harrison inquired in a dry tone as he glanced around for signs of the alleged victim.

Amanda scowled at him. "He was here less than a half-hour ago, draped right over that tombstone. I heard the shot, then I saw him." She didn't mention that she'd also touched him, since she'd been told specifically not to do so.

"Could have been faked to get your attention."

"He was definitely dead."

"You're a coroner now, too?"

"Dead is dead. I've seen my share of homicide victims, the same as you. Would you make a mistake about something like that?"

"Not likely," he agreed.

"Well, then."

The detective studied her intently, then nodded. "Maybe you'd better start at the beginning," he said.

He was displaying astonishing patience given the fact that he'd hauled a goodly number of Atlanta police officers out on what certainly appeared to be a wild goose chase. Amanda took heart from the fact that he hadn't sent a single person away from the scene.

She gave him a brief summary of the call to *Inside Atlanta*, leaving out the specifics of the alleged crime. When she was finished, Harrison regarded her suspiciously.

"That's it? Some man called the office, promised information on a story, and you raced out to the cemetery at midnight?"

"That's about it."

"I don't believe it: Either your social life isn't what it could be or there's something you're not telling me."

"Why couldn't it be that simple? You know a good reporter checks out every lead."

"Amanda, you stopped chasing ambulances a long time ago. When you get tips, they generally involve major corruption, political scandals. You don't go snooping around town at midnight, hoping to find out if some average guy took a couple of bets on last Sunday's Falcons' game."

"This man called the office. I didn't even talk to him myself. Oscar did and he believed the guy. He claimed to have a story, and, okay," she admitted grudgingly, "it was potentially a big story. I don't have enough of the details to go into it. I don't even have an inside source anymore."

"Inside what?" he said, leaping on that tidbit of information with as much alacrity as Donelli might have in days gone by.

"Do this," she suggested, skirting the question. "Have your guys go over that area. If the man was shot—which he was, then there should be blood—which I saw. Nobody had time to wash things down after that. I can't even imagine how they managed to snatch the guy. Anyway, if you find traces of blood, maybe some male footprints, then you'll have to believe the possibility that a murder was committed, even without the body."

Jim Harrison regarded her closely for several seconds, then waved to his crime scene technicians. When they came over, he instructed them to look for any evidence that someone might have been shot and then carted away. Amanda wanted very badly to follow them as they set up spotlights and went to work. Instead, the detective was gesturing toward his car. It was less a come-hither motion than a haul-ass one.

"Let's go over this one more time for the record," he suggested when they were settled in the front seat of his unmarked police car, surrounded by gum wrappers and empty Styrofoam coffee cups. Amanda kicked aside a few diet-soda cans as she tried to find room for her feet.

"Should I call a lawyer?" she inquired.

"Not unless you have this alleged victim stuffed in the trunk of your car. I can have someone check, if you like."

"Not necessary."

Jim Harrison was very good at what he did, probably in part because he looked so disappointed when her answers didn't please him. That weary, sorrowful expression made her want to spill everything, but the promise of that exposé kept her silent. She said no more than she absolutely had to. She justified her reticence by telling herself there was no point in wasting tax dollars investigating something that might have been a figment of the vanished murder victim's imagination.

A young technician with a blond crewcut and an all-American face approached the car. He looked about the right age to be peddling tickets for a fraternity fund-raiser, not to be given the responsibility for collecting murder clues. Harrison rolled down the window.

"Hey, Ken, what do you have?"

"I can't be sure, but it could be blood," he said with scientific caution. "Won't know for certain if it is, or if it's human, until we run some tests. I'd say there was definitely somebody there and recently, too. This substance isn't dry. The moss on that tombstone was all slicked down, too, as if something heavy might have slid over it."

Amanda shot a triumphant look at the detective. "A body, for example?"

Ken shrugged. "Could be," he said noncommittally.

"Any footprints?" Harrison asked. "The ground's fairly soft. Should have some nice ones."

"Right. Quite a few in fact. We're getting molds now. I'd say three separate sets. The victim's and two more, one male, one female, judging by the size of the impressions."

It was not Amanda's imagination that Jim Harrison immediately glanced down at her feet. She found the quick guesswork a little insulting, despite the telltale mud on her shoes.

"One set about that size, by any chance?" he asked the technician.

Ken leaned in the window, glanced down, studied Amanda's sneakers, and nodded. He appeared startled by Harrison's accuracy. "Looks like the right kind of tread, too."

It was Harrison's turn to look triumphant. "Thanks, Ken."

When the technician had gone back to work, Harrison turned slowly back to Amanda. "Well?"

"You don't think I threw him over my shoulder and dragged him out of here, do you?"

"No, but I'd be mighty fascinated to hear what you did do."

"I checked for ID," she admitted reluctantly. "That's all."

"And maybe a little evidence that he claimed to have?"

"Okay, yes. But he didn't have a thing on him. I swear it. Not even car keys. Either he lied about the evidence he had with him and came in empty-handed or they stripped him."

"Did you hear a car after you arrived?"

"No, but he might have gotten here first and waited. Or he could have parked outside the cemetery and walked in."

"Did you hear a car after you checked the body?"

"No. Not until you all drove in."

"So, how'd the killer get here and how did he haul the victim away?"

Amanda shrugged. "Good question."

"I suppose he might have waited around, hoping you'd be so terrified you'd run."

Amanda considered the implications. "You mean he could still be here in the cemetery?"

"Doubtful, but you never know. Only the main gate's open at this hour and you didn't see him use that. I'll send some of the patrol cars around to check the roads inside here for parked cars.''

It occurred to Amanda that it might be worthwhile to check the cars on the outside perimeter of the cemetery as well. Of course, most of them probably belonged to folks who lived in the neighborhood, but one might belong to the murder victim. After checking for a few days straight to see which cars moved, it might be possible to identify one as having been abandoned. Unless she got lucky, it would be tedious, but it might be the best shot she had at identifying her mysterious and now very dead and missing source.

The sooner she got started on that, the better. She wasn't likely to learn any more from the police investigation here tonight.

"You need me for anything else?" she asked Harrison.

"No. You can go." His gaze narrowed. "I suppose it's too much to hope that you're going to drive straight out to the country at a respectable, law-abiding speed and get a good night's sleep."

"You can always hope." There was no point in telling Jim Harrison that she hadn't had a good night's sleep since the scheduled day of her wedding. She missed sharing her bed and her sleepy, late-night thoughts with Donelli. She would have given almost anything to be able to toss around tonight's events with him, maybe even lure him into helping with the investigation.

That kind of longing, however, was a waste of energy, she scolded herself as she drew a sketchy map of the streets surrounding the cemetery. Then with weary determination she set out to place every single car in the neighborhood on the crudely drawn map.

Most of the cars in the lower-middle-class neighborhood were in driveways, but there were at least fifty on the surrounding streets. She put stars by the tag numbers of a couple that looked flashy enough to belong to a young man on the move. She would watch those more closely than the others.

Amanda was on her way out of the vicinity when she noted the rental car bumper sticker on a nondescript sedan parked about two blocks from the cemetery's main entrance. There were no houses nearby, only a dark schoolyard and a handful of neighborhood stores. All in all, it was an odd place for a tourist to have parked in the middle of the night. She took down the tag number and the rental car ID number. If her source was genuinely skittish about the conspiracy he'd stumbled onto at the bank, maybe he would have rented a car for tonight's meeting to avoid being followed. It might be a long shot, but she didn't have any short leads anyway. It was worth checking out.

Impatient as always, she called the rental car company on her car phone as she headed home, staying dutifully under the speed limit until she was out of Detective Harrison's jurisdiction.

"That's not the kind of information we can give out," a bored clerk told her when she asked who had rented the car.

"Look, the car was parked near my house and I'm afraid I tagged the bumper when I cut the corner too short. The damage is minor, but I don't want this poor guy to have to pay for something I did."

"You could come in here and file a report."

"And have it on the record? No way. Insurance rates are tough enough as it is. I'd rather just square it with the guy who rented the car. You know how it is."

Apparently the young man could relate to the concept

of skyrocketing insurance premiums and sly deals to beat the system. "Okay, I'll check it out for you, but don't spread it around how you got this information."

"Of course not."

She waited while he apparently pushed the appropriate buttons on some highly efficient computer.

"Where'd you say this accident took place?"

"Actually I didn't say. Why?"

"Because the local address on the rental agreement doesn't sound right."

"Oh? Why not?"

"I know the area and the only thing this could be is that cemetery out there."

Amanda's heart thumped with anticipation. "That is the area where I ran into the car. About two blocks away, in fact. When was the car rented?"

"About six months ago. It's in a minilease program."

Now that was a surprise, Amanda thought. Could she have been wrong about it belonging to her source, rather than to someone in the neighborhood? "Is there a name on the agreement?"

"Sure is, but I wouldn't trust it. If the guy'd give a fake address, why not a fake name?"

"Because he'd have to show his driver's license, wouldn't he? He could always explain away the address discrepancy by saying he'd just moved."

"Yeah, right. Anyway, the name is Howell. Richard Howell. I don't know how you'll find him, though. Maybe you'd better just leave a note on his windshield."

*Or tacked onto the family vault in the cemetery,* Amanda thought. "Thanks. I'll do that. You've been a big help."

As she hung up, she thought about Richard Howell.

What macabre sense of humor had led him to put down the cemetery as his address? Unless the name was pure coincidence, there was a certain bitter irony at play here. He'd been shot to death within spitting distance of where he would no doubt be buried when his identity caught up with him downtown and his body was located.

In the meantime, though, she was several steps ahead of the police. That meant that if she got to work first thing in the morning, she might be able to come up with sufficient information on Richard Howell to start checking out the story he'd told her and Oscar.

Obviously, in addition to that bizarre sense of humor, he'd been idealistic and well intentioned—all traits that appealed to her. There weren't a lot of folks like that left in the world. She figured she owed it to him to see that he hadn't died in vain.

# CHAPTER

## *Three*

**D**EAD men tell no tales, but sometimes cemetery files say quite a lot. And, unlike policemen, the Department of Motor Vehicles, and other official entities, cemetery managers were rarely asked a lot of questions about their clientele. Amanda decided to pay a visit to the office of the Eternal Peace Garden of Souls to see what she could learn about the Howells. With any luck at all, she could prove it was more than sheer coincidence that Richard Howell had chosen the Howell vault as their meeting place.

Indeed, Mrs. Mabel Franklin, who lived with her husband, Lucas, on the cemetery grounds in a squat little brick house, could hardly wait to chat over a cup of tea. She and Amanda waited for Lucas to return from a final check of a newly dug burial plot that had turned over a fresh slash of Georgia's finest red clay.

"Lucas likes to oversee these things himself," Mrs. Franklin said. "Can't count on getting good help these days, you know. Besides, when folks show up for the burial, there's already plenty of stress going around without having some awful snafu marring the solemn occasion."

"I'm sure you're a big help to him, too," Amanda said, with more hope than generosity. A talkative source wasn't a big help, if he or she didn't have any secrets to share.

"I like to do my part, keep things tidy in the office, don't you know," she said, displaying a look of humility that belied the pride in her voice. "Do a bit of filing now and again, when the secretary gets behind."

"How long have you been the overseers here?"

"Lucas took over back in eighty-one, I believe it was. He'd worked for one of the funeral homes in town for nearly thirty-five years. Saw to many a fine burial. He began to think about retiring, but with costs the way they are these days, we knew we'd be wanting a little extra. Taking over here, with the house provided and all, seemed like the thing to do. Our kids think it's downright strange, us living in a cemetery, but it suits us just fine. Don't have to worry about noisy neighbors now, do we?" she said with a dry chuckle.

Amanda managed a halfhearted smile in recognition of what Mrs. Franklin obviously considered a clever joke. "Do you and Mr. Franklin make it a point to be familiar with the grounds? Do you recall who's buried in which plots?"

"Oh my, absolutely," she said as she poured a fresh cup of tea and offered a plate of homemade peanut-butter cookies. "You never know when some long-lost family member will show up, asking to see the burial site of a relative. Have to be able to direct 'em straight to it. Won't do to fumble around like some nincompoop. Word like that gets around, don't you know. Gives people peace of mind to think that someone's here looking after their dearly departed. Our brochure promises perpetual care, and that's just what we give."

"I'm sure you do. I drove through the grounds just recently and noticed some fine old family markers here. The Howell vault, for example."

Her eyes lit up. "Oh my, yes. That is a beauty, isn't it? Quite old, too. Four, maybe five generations buried in there. Lucas would know for certain."

She leaned forward conspiratorially, until Amanda could see the woman's pink scalp beneath her wisps of blue-tinted white hair. "Quite a history in that family," she said. "Are you familiar with it?"

Amanda shook her head.

"Well, they say one of the Howell girls suffered a tragic loss. Back in the fifties, I believe it was. The eighteen-fifties, that is. The kids around here swear they've seen her walking through the graveyard late at night, still looking for her young man. Never seen her myself, but that doesn't mean she's not there."

Amanda tried to contain her skepticism since the woman clearly found the sad story both fascinating and entirely plausible. "I see."

"Funny you asking about the Howells," Mrs. Franklin said, smoothing her housedress over her ample lap. "I was just thinking about them the other day—day before yesterday, in fact."

"Why was that?"

"We had a call from someone asking exactly where the vault was. Said he hadn't been there in a while and didn't want to be bothered by stopping by for a map. I told this man right off, of course, but it surprised me."

"Why?"

"Because I thought they'd all died out when Mrs. Jessica Lynn Howell went a few years ago. Saddest funeral I ever saw. Lucas and I were the only ones there, except for the minister we called in to say a few words. Her attorney insisted that's the way she wanted it, with no fuss. Wasn't even an announcement in the newspaper till after she was in the vault."

Amanda swallowed her disappointment. "Mrs. Howell had no children?"

"There was talk of a son at the time her husband died, but from the nervous way she talked about him, I gathered he'd disappeared long ago with no love lost between him and his father. There was quite a bit of money in that family, so you'd think the boy would have come back for that, if nothing else. I suppose it's to his credit that he didn't."

"Perhaps he'd been cut out of the will, if he was estranged from his father."

"Perhaps. I just had the feeling he was gone for good, maybe even dead."

"You don't happen to recall his name, do you?"

She tapped her lower lip with a short, blunt-tipped nail painted an astonishing shade of fire-engine red that clashed dramatically with her flowered pink housedress. "Let me see now. The father's name was Randolph, but this wasn't a junior. Robert maybe? No. No. Richard." Her faded blue eyes lit up. "That was it. Richard."

Hallelujah! Unfortunately, Amanda had the distinct impression that she'd reached the end of Mrs. Franklin's knowledge about the Howells. At least about the youngest generation. She thanked her profusely for her time.

Mrs. Franklin looked extremely disappointed that the gabfest was ending. "Are you sure you wouldn't like to stay to speak with Lucas?"

"No, really. You've been very helpful."

Amanda was almost out the door when she thought of one last thing: "You don't happen to recall what the family business might have been, do you?"

"Why of course," she said. "I'm surprised you don't recognize the name. I thought everyone in Atlanta knew the Howells, but then again you don't sound like you're from around these parts." She paused expectantly.

"New York, actually."

"I knew it. I said to myself when you first came in, now here's somebody from up north. Never been to New York myself. Too uncivilized. At any rate, the Howells were very prominent in banking circles. Mrs. Howell sold out after her husband died. They had fifty, maybe a hundred branches all around the state by then. Merged with one of those big out-of-state banks. From California, I think."

She paused thoughtfully. "Or maybe it was North Carolina. Anyway, they have a lovely building right downtown. Thirty floors, if you can imagine that. Why, I can recall when the main office was an old brick house on Peachtree. It's gone now, of course. They call that progress," she said with a sad shake of her head. "Ripping down people's memories is what I say."

Amanda was far less interested in the height of the Howells' former bank building than she was in what it suggested about young Richard. If indeed her source had been the disinherited son, chances were extremely good that he would have had sufficient expertise to detect a major shift of funds in an illegal arms deal. Now all she had to do was figure out which bank was involved.

It was nearly eleven when she finally got to the *Inside Atlanta* offices. Jenny Lee practically leaped from behind the reception desk to embrace her.

"Amanda, honey, where have you been? Oscar's been frantic. He's been in and out of Joel's office half-a-dozen times trying to decide what to do. And that Detective Harrison's been calling every fifteen minutes. Oscar was all ready to call Donelli and have him go over and check on you."

At Amanda's horrified expression, Jenny Lee soothed, "Now, now, don't get yourself all worked up. I stopped him. I knew how you'd feel about that. But what on earth is going on? I was about ready to drive out to your house myself. You're never this late."

"It's a long story."

"I've got time."

"Considering the number of blinking lights on the phone, I don't think you do. Not if you intend to keep your job anyway. Is Oscar in his office?"

"Yes—unless he's gone back up to Joel's to wear out the carpet in there again."

Joel Crenshaw was the magazine's publisher and the man responsible for luring both Amanda and Oscar away from the rural weekly where she'd begun her pathetic career in Georgia. She owed Joel big-time for saving her sanity, if not for putting her professional life back at the level it had been in New York. Amanda hoped Oscar had not gotten Joel all riled up about her absence. Joel was capable of pulling strings straight up to the governor's mansion. Amanda hated to see contacts like that wasted. She really would have to start carrying her beeper again.

Fortunately, she found Oscar in his own office. Unfortunately, Joel was with him. So was Detective Harrison. Jenny Lee, damn her, hadn't mentioned that he'd shown up to give a personal assist in the supposed crisis.

"Where the hell have you been?" they asked in a chorus.

"Nice harmony," she declared. "You guys should think of going on the road."

Oscar scowled. The publisher looked relieved. Detective Harrison seemed slightly confused.

"I thought you'd vanished," he said, glancing from her to Oscar and back again.

"You didn't show up. You didn't call," Oscar grumbled defensively.

"I'm working on a story, or had you forgotten?"

"Maybe I did. It's been so long," he snapped, the worry lines just now easing out of his brow.

Amanda winced. "I'm sorry. I didn't mean to get everyone all worked up. As you can see, I'm just fine. I was just checking out a lead."

"Story panning out the way you hoped?" Joel asked at once, a gleam in his eyes.

"Could be," she said cautiously. If she showed any more enthusiasm, he'd demand it for the next issue, and she wasn't about to rush this through to a sloppy conclusion. Besides, Harrison was watching her far too closely. Obviously he had his own suspicions about what she'd been up to.

"Guess I'll just have to wait like everyone else," Joel said with a shrug. "Well, if everything's under control here, I'll go see what I can do about convincing our advertisers to beef up their presence for this major exposé we'll have coming in the next issue or so. Think I'll tell 'em we can figure on a lot of national play, bigger print run, wider distribution. Keep up the good work."

Amanda groaned. "I didn't say anything about a major exposé."

He grinned. "You didn't have to. Oscar did." He shook the detective's hand. "Good to see you, Jim."

When he was gone, the chorus demanding to know what she'd been up to was reduced to two. They were both emphatic in their requests for information. Since there was no way around it aside from bolting for the door, she gave them a short version of her activities since leaving the cemetery the night before.

"You have an ID on the victim?" Harrison demanded incredulously.

"It's not positive, but I'd say it's a damned good guess. Richard Howell."

"Of the banking Howells?" the detective asked. "Of course. What am I thinking of? The murder took place right at their family vault. Has to be that family or a damned weird coincidence." His conviction changed to puzzlement. "But I thought he'd disappeared years ago."

"Maybe he did," Amanda said. "Maybe he came back. We won't know for sure until we can find something more on him—where he lived, where he worked, whether he's even missing. I'd settle for an old family photo, so I can compare it to the dead man I saw last night. Just because there was a car in the neighborhood rented by a Richard Howell doesn't prove that's who was killed in the cemetery or that he's related to the banking family."

Amanda offered the touch of reason to keep all of them from leaping to wild conclusions just because they made pieces of the puzzle fit more neatly. Although she wasn't enthusiastic about sharing her investigation with the police, it made sense to try and strike a bargain that could save them both a lot of time.

"Why don't I see if Howell worked for any of the banks in town. It would be a natural for him to turn up at one of them. I'll let you know if I have any luck."

Harrison smiled ruefully. "How nice. And what would you like the police to do to assist in your investigation?"

Ignoring the sarcasm, she said, "I'm sure you have your ways to track down where he lived."

"Or lives," he corrected.

She nodded. "Or lives."

Jim Harrison stood up, shoved his hands in his pockets, and gave her one last scowl. "I can't stop you from making those calls, but I want to know what you find out."

"You'll be the first . . ." She caught sight of Oscar's disapproving glare, then corrected herself: "You'll be the second to know."

Harrison shot a pointed look at both of them. "I trust the time lag won't be significant."

"Not if yours isn't," she said agreeably. She winked at Oscar as she slipped past the detective and went to her desk.

An hour later Amanda was totally absorbed in the listing of foreign banks in the Atlanta Yellow Pages, when she heard Jenny Lee exclaim, "Why, you're Amanda's mama! I'm so glad to meet you."

In her haste to spin around to face the reception area, Amanda almost flew off the seat of her chair. There, indeed, looking somewhat uncertain, stood her mother, suitcases stacked around her. A lot of suitcases, she noted with a sinking sensation.

Amanda cast one last, longing look at the phone book, then hurried across the newsroom, trying to hide her shock and dismay. She hoped she was successful. Her mother looked as if she'd already had more than she could take.

"Mother, what on earth are you doing in Atlanta?" she asked, embracing the tall, stiff woman.

She was struck by how frail her mother appeared. She took a good long look at her. Her usually lively blue eyes were shadowed, her always tidy frosted hair was mussed. Whatever makeup she'd put on before leaving New York had long since worn away. Only a crisis of monumental proportions would bring her mother out of the house, much less halfway down the east coast in this condition. Amanda didn't like the implications any more than she liked that pile of suitcases.

"Why didn't you call and let me know you were coming?" she asked, drawing her mother into the newsroom and urging her to sit down. She noticed that her mother didn't even glance around—another bad sign. She usually had plenty to say about the decor of her surroundings, plus almost as much curiosity as Amanda had.

"I'm sorry, dear," she said in a lackluster tone. "I suppose it was something of a last-minute impulse. There seems to be a lot of that going around in the family these days," she added enigmatically. "I hope I'm not interrupting anything important."

"Nothing that can't wait a few minutes while you tell me what you're doing here," Amanda said. "Just let me get my things and we'll go have a cup of coffee. How long are you staying?"

Her mother evaded her eyes. "Actually we need to talk about that."

Amanda didn't like the sound of that either. Under the best of conditions she and her mother could manage a civil weekend. Longer would definitely be a test, especially when she was right in the middle of a breaking story. Her mother had never entirely approved of her career choice, despite the fact that Amanda had clearly inherited her need to poke around in dark corners from her mother. If she discovered that Amanda had spent the preceding night in a cemetery and that her companion had been shot, she'd be lecturing until the wee hours of the morning. Amanda wasn't up to it.

"Let's forget the coffee. I'll drive you out to the house so you can get settled." Maybe on the drive she'd be able to get straight answers.

"You needn't interrupt your schedule for me. I could wait for you," her mother said in a tone suggestive of martyrdom.

That tone, in fact everything about this visit, was entirely out of character. Amanda's sense of alarm grew.

"Absolutely not," she told her mother firmly. "I'll just get my purse." She saw that Jenny Lee had trailed them into the newsroom and was hovering anxiously. "Jenny Lee, could you start calling those banks I've marked? I've done the first two. See if you can find out if a Richard Howell works there or if anyone's failed to show up for work the last two days."

The receptionist looked pleased by the assignment, but skeptical. "What makes you think they'll tell me something like that?"

"They won't, at least not intentionally. But I'm sure you can find some way to sweet-talk them out of the information. If worse comes to worse, tell them you're looking for a job and ask if there are any openings."

Amanda saw her mother's eyes widen disapprovingly.

"Darling, isn't that dishonest?"

"It depends on exactly what Jenny Lee tells them, doesn't it?" Amanda responded briskly. "Now let's go. I can't wait to hear all about this surprise visit. Tell me the truth. How long are you planning to stay?"

Her mother continued to avoid her gaze, which Amanda considered yet another bad sign. A very bad sign, indeed.

"Mother?"

"Actually, dear, that's what I wanted to discuss with you," she said with obviously forced cheer. "If things work out, I could be here permanently."

# CHAPTER

## *Four*

"**P**ERMANENTLY?**"** Amanda repeated weakly, very nearly driving her car into a ditch. When she was back on the highway, she dared a glance at her mother. "You and Dad are moving to Atlanta? When did you decide that?"

"I didn't say a word about your father," her mother said stiffly.

Shock spread through Amanda as she began to get an inkling of what this visit was about. Who was she kidding? She'd had her suspicions the minute she'd seen all those suitcases. She just hadn't wanted to admit it.

"Mother, what on earth is going on?" She flatly refused to mention the word *divorce*. She didn't even want to hint at it.

"Your father and I have separated," her mother said far more bluntly than Amanda would have preferred.

She couldn't have been more astonished if her mother had announced that Long Island had sunk into the sea, leaving her adrift and homeless. Before she could react, however, her always calm, always controlled mother burst into tears. It was the only time, other than at her grandmother Hunt's funeral, that Amanda had seen Elisa Hunt Bailey cry.

She felt her eyes begin to sting as dismay and confusion settled in. What the hell had been going on up in New York over the last few months? Had both of her parents lost their senses? The last she'd heard, her father was still recuperating from a heart attack. That illness had prevented them from coming to Atlanta for the wedding that, as it turned out at the last second, hadn't happened. She'd been glad they hadn't been there for the debacle. In retrospect, however, she wished they'd made the trip so she could have seen for herself what sort of strain their marriage was under.

Uncertain, totally at a loss for words, and suddenly feeling awkward in the unexpected role of comforter, Amanda found a place to pull over and stopped the car. She gathered her distraught mother in a hug.

"It's going to be okay," Amanda murmured, even as she was struck by the absurdity of the reassurance, given the circumstances. How many people had uttered those same empty words to her over the last couple of months? Besides, until she knew exactly what had happened, she had absolutely no way of knowing if or when everything might be all right again. Her own life was a prime example of exactly how muddled and complicated the relationship between the sexes could become.

*But not after thirty-five years*, she cried inside. Some *things in a person's life are supposed to remain stable and certain.*

Still, the falsely placating words she'd uttered seemed to have calmed her mother.

"I'm sorry, dear," she said, dabbing daintily at her eyes with what Amanda knew had started the day as a crisp, white, lace-edged hankie, one of the dozens Grandmother Hunt had doled out as gifts over the years. Now it was a damp, wrinkled mess. "I don't know what's come over me."

Even though she wanted to demand an explanation of the insanity that had split her parents apart after all those years of marriage, Amanda bit back her questions.

"I'll fix a nice cup of tea when we get home and we'll talk this out," she promised as she pulled back onto the highway. "I'm sure there's been some dreadful mistake. You and Dad love each other. I know you do."

"I always thought so," her mother said sadly, then settled back into the passenger seat of Amanda's car. She stared out the window and said not another word the entire way home.

The silence gave Amanda time to try to deal with the hysteria building inside her. She was barely keeping a grip on her own sanity these days. How was she supposed to console her mother, patch up her parents' marriage, solve this murder, prove that a banking scandal had indeed taken place, and fix up her own life, all at the same time? That was the sort of pressure that landed people in institutions.

Oh, well, she had always considered herself at her best in a crisis. It appeared she was about to be tested.

* * *

Given the shaky status of her ability to cope with anything these days, Amanda thought it was probably just as well that her mother firmly turned down the offer of tea and a chat. She lugged her belongings into the guest room, drew the drapes, and pleaded exhaustion.

"I know you're anxious to get back to work, dear. I'll be fine."

It was definitely a dismissal. Amanda regarded the stoic expression on her mother's face and felt like crying. "I'm not sure . . ."

"Go, darling. There's no point in your sitting around here while I nap. We'll have plenty of time to talk." She gave Amanda a wobbly smile. "Just think how wonderful it will be being together again. We can get to know each other on a whole different level, as friends, instead of mother and daughter."

That, of course, was exactly what Amanda was hoping to avoid. She wanted this crisis averted and her mother on the first plane back to New York. She wanted a mother and a father, not a new best friend. It appeared, however, that she would not get her wish today.

"I'll call you later and let you know what time I'll be home," she promised.

"Thank you, dear. That would be very considerate. Now run along before you get in trouble with your boss."

Since there was nothing to be gained by hanging around, Amanda left. As she made her way back to the highway, she grappled with the concept of her parents' marriage being on the rocks. The abrupt fissure of an earthquake made more sense to her, and she'd barely passed geology.

Elisa Hunt and Nelson Bailey had met in grammar school. There had never been a question in anyone's mind that they would wed the minute they were old enough. The family album was crammed with photos of the two of them at various ages—chubby-cheeked and filthy at six, awkward and gangly at thirteen, shyly in love at sixteen, and radiating joy and contentment on their wedding day at twenty-one.

The constancy of their love had been the steadying influence throughout Amanda's life. It had also made her own failures in relationships that much more devastating. Though she'd never admitted it—not even to herself until now—she wanted what her parents had. If she'd had to label their relationship she might have called them true soul-mates.

She thought she'd found that elusive compatibility with Donelli. She thought she'd found a man who could provide a balance to her impetuosity without smothering her, a man who understood her ambition and her commitment to the search for truth beneath the tangled lies of politicians, a man of strength and high ideals.

Without even realizing what she was doing, she found herself driving past his farm on her way back to Atlanta. It took every bit of her resolve to keep from turning into the long driveway. However, that reticence to make the first move toward a reconciliation didn't prevent her from pulling onto the shoulder of the two-lane road and searching the landscape for some sign of him. The fields were lying fallow, though, and everything was still. He was probably inside.

Maybe he was even working on a case, now that he'd finally taken the steps necessary to become a private investigator. If nothing else had come of their time together, she was glad that she'd encouraged him not to let all his experience as a Brooklyn cop go to waste. He'd been burned out when he'd left the force, but he had a quick, savvy intellect that had no business being wasted on growing tomatoes and killing garden pests.

She forced back a sigh of regret, shifted into gear, and drove on. It took thirty minutes and as many miles before she could refocus her attention on the investigation. By the time she got back to the office, she had a mental list of half a dozen things to be done to check out Richard Howell if the police hadn't already come up with something. Since there was no officially declared murder on the books, she doubted if they were even half as motivated to find answers as she was.

As she stepped off the elevator, Jenny Lee began waving a slip of paper in her direction, all the while chatting with a girlfriend on the phone.

"Gotta go," she said in a rush. She leaped to her feet and followed Amanda into the newsroom, ignoring the blinking switchboard.

"This has gotta be the bank, Amanda," she said, turning over the paper. "The woman got real nervous when I started asking questions. I'll bet if I went down there, I could prove it. I could maybe ask one of the tellers or something. Tell 'em I was a friend of Richard's. You said he looked like he was in his twenties. I could even be his girlfriend. Pretend I was real worried because he hadn't come home."

Amanda knew how anxious Jenny Lee was to be promoted to full-time reporter, but there was one serious risk in her scheme. If Richard Howell was still very much alive and at work, the appearance of a woman pretending to be his girlfriend might backfire.

"Exactly what did you ask the woman at this bank?" She glanced at the slip of paper. "National Bank, N.V., the Netherlands, right?"

"Yeah. I checked. Anyway, I said I was trying to

reach Richard Howell and asked if he worked there. She wanted to know who I was. I said I was calling to confirm his employment because he'd applied for a loan.''

Amanda winced. "Jenny Lee, the man worked for a bank. They probably give out employee loans all the time and take the payments straight out of their paychecks.''

Jenny Lee regarded her indignantly. "I'm not totally stupid, Amanda. I said it was a manufacturer loan for a new car, zero percent financing. Surely they wouldn't be able to match that. I even threw in the name of a dealership to make it sound legitimate. You know Johnny Lou Tatum's always promoting these slick, fancy deals at his showrooms over in Gwinnett.''

"Okay, I'm sorry. You covered all the bases," she conceded. "What did she say?''

"Just that she'd have to check with the bank manager before giving out any information. Now it seems to me that it should be routine to confirm employment unless there's something shady going on, right?''

"It's possible.''

"So, can I go and check it out? Don't forget I actually do have bank experience.''

Jenny Lee's father owned a small bank in a rural town on the Georgia-Florida border. She'd grown up around piles of money that didn't belong to her. If she'd ever been tempted to claim some for her own, she'd never confessed it to Amanda.

"I know you're qualified, but let's think this through a minute. I don't want you blundering over there until we have a plan.''

"But you'll let me be the one to go, right? You'll work it out with Oscar, like you did last time?''

Jenny Lee's enthusiasm was so reminiscent of her own a few years back that Amanda never had been able to say no to her. Besides, Oscar had promised months ago that he would try to create an opening for her on the reporting staff. The only thing holding him back was the fear that he wouldn't find a decent receptionist to replace her. A string of extraordinarily inept temps had confirmed his worst fears.

"I'll talk to Oscar. Now, has Jim Harrison called in with any information on Howell?"

"Not yet."

"Then let's make a few more phone calls. You have a friend at the phone company, don't you?"

"I wouldn't call Lucy a friend exactly, but she helped me when we were having trouble getting all these phone lines installed for the new system. We've stayed in touch."

"Good. Try information first, though. See if Richard Howell has a listing. I checked the phone directory earlier and he wasn't in that, but he could be unlisted. If he is, call her. I want the number and, if possible, the address."

"Got it," Jenny Lee said. "What are you going to do?"

"Check out this bank in the data files. I might even call the ever-friendly FBI and ask a few questions. I figure Jeffrey Dunne owes me after that stunt he and Donelli pulled."

It took less than ten minutes to determine that the National Bank of the Netherlands had not been at the center of any reported controversies in the past couple of years. There had, however, been a Dutch company tied in with the Banca Nazionale del Lavoro scandal. In July of '92 the firm had pled guilty to charges of violating U.S. laws that restricted the transfer of U.S.-origin military technology to Iraq. An interesting sidelight, but hardly proof of a direct connection with a bank from the Netherlands.

Reluctant to open old wounds, Amanda took her time placing the call to Jeffrey Dunne. Naturally the special agent was out of the office. That seemed to be the official response even if he happened to be standing within inches of the person answering the phone. Just one of the little power gambits he liked to play. It meant he got to call back in his own sweet time.

"Just tell him Amanda Roberts called and that I'm treading on federal turf again. That ought to pique his interest. Read that back to me, please. I want to be sure he gets the entire message exactly."

The secretary seemed startled rather than insulted by the request. She repeated the message verbatim. *Naturally*, Amanda thought grumpily. Jeffrey Dunne wouldn't tolerate inefficiency or inaccuracy.

"When are you expecting to hear from him?" Amanda asked, knowing better than to expect a straight answer.

"He checks in regularly."

"Regularly as in hourly, regularly as in twice a day, once a month, what?" The surliness in her tone made her cringe. It wasn't this poor woman's fault that Jeffrey Dunne stood for a long list of things that drove Amanda crazy. "Sorry. Just have him call."

Fortunately for her overall mood, Jenny Lee was standing by her desk when she hung up. She had a triumphant expression on her face.

"You got it," Amanda guessed.

"Phone number and address," Jenny Lee confirmed.

Amanda grabbed her purse. "Let's go."

They were halfway to the elevator when Oscar popped his head out of his office. "Going someplace?"

"To check out Richard Howell's residence."

"Both of you?" he said with a pointed look at Jenny Lee.

"She tracked him down. She deserves to come along," Amanda said.

"And the phones? Last I heard I was paying her to answer them."

"Turn on the automatic voice mail machine," Amanda shot right back. "It says the office closes at five. It's nearly that now."

"Four-thirty is not five o'clock. Besides, you hate those machines."

Amanda shrugged. "I hate 'em when I get lost in voice mail hell. Around here, it has its uses."

Oscar took note of Jenny Lee's hopeful expression and Amanda's stubborn one and in a rare mood of generosity waved them on. "Get out of here. I'll answer the damn phones myself."

Jenny Lee beamed. "Thanks, boss."

"Go. Try to stay out of trouble. The thought of the two of you on the loose together is enough to get my ulcer acting up again. See that you report in before I have an honest-to-God attack."

# CHAPTER

## *Five*

RICHARD Howell's address was in Grant Park, about three miles east of downtown Atlanta. Grant Park was an area in transition. Once the stately homes had belonged to the wealthy. Then slowly the area had become rundown and undesirable. Now, a combination of historic pride and the desire for close-in accommodations had resulted in renewed attempts to gentrify the area. Not nearly as far along as Miami Beach's Art Deco district or Savannah's historical center, it promised to be far more than it had yet delivered. For every one spruced-up house, there were two more that were deserted and ramshackle.

A developer would need vision and deep pockets to invest in the redevelopment of the area, Amanda decided as they drove into the neighborhood. An individual would have to be idealistic, artistic, determined, or some combination of the three. It might help if he owned a gun and knew how to use it.

Although it was still daylight when they reached Howell's street, Jenny Lee was glancing around nervously. "Maybe we should have called Larry and asked him to come along." Then, as if unwilling to admit that she was afraid, she added, "To take pictures, I mean."

"There will be plenty of time for that later," Amanda said. To salvage her friend's pride, she ignored Jenny Lee's unspoken fears.

Amanda pulled into a parking place half a block from the address Jenny Lee had given her. It was in the middle of a block of houses with spacious lawns, most of them overgrown with weeds. While the other houses were in various stages of repair, Howell's had been sandblasted to reveal a lovely, aged pink brick. The shutters had been painted back. The brass outdoor light fixture had been polished to a soft gleam. The light was on, though it was just now twilight.

"What do you think that means?" Jenny Lee asked, pointing to the light.

"Could be he's gone out for the evening and left a light burning."

"Or it might have been on ever since he left to meet you last night."

Amanda nodded. "Definitely a possibility."

"I'm getting a real bad feeling about this," Jenny Lee said, scanning the neighborhood for signs of activity and not liking what she saw.

"Why? If that was Richard Howell in the cemetery last night, we already know he's dead."

"Are you forgetting that his body disappeared? What if they brought him back and dumped him in here? Don't tell me that hasn't crossed your mind, Amanda."

"Yes, it's crossed my mind, but we won't know anything if we don't check it out. Come on." She led the way to the front door and knocked loudly. The only hint of sound inside seemed to be coming from a radio or stereo tuned to classical music. Amanda knocked again.

"Now what?" Jenny Lee asked. Her eyes widened when Amanda tested the doorknob. "Amanda, you can't just go walking into a stranger's house."

Amanda ignored the protest. "Damn, it's locked. Let's go around to the back. There's bound to be some sort of entrance back there."

Jenny Lee shivered. "I don't like this."

"So you've said."

Amanda walked around the corner checking out the windows that were just above street level. Only one light was burning downstairs. That, combined with the music, seemed to indicate that someone had just gone out for the evening. But which evening?

There was a brick wall around the backyard with a high wooden gate. The gate was latched from the inside but not locked. Amanda reached over and unlatched it. The gate opened onto a small yard. A neat brick patio edged by flower beds was tucked against the back of the house. Chrysanthemums had been blooming until just recently. Suddenly she was reminded of the dead chrysanthemums at the Howell vault last night. What if they'd been taken from this garden, not ages ago as she'd suspected, but on a more recent visit? Perhaps shortly after Mabel Franklin had taken that mysterious phone call about the location of the vault? It made sense.

She checked out the rest of the surroundings. An empty beer bottle sat on a glass-topped table, as if someone had recently sat there to relax. A yuppie, fond of the latest import. That fit, too.

There were French doors leading to the inside. Those, too, were locked.

"He's obviously not here," Jenny Lee said, her arms clenched around her middle as if to ward off a chill, though the evening was balmy. "Let's go before it gets dark."

"In a minute," Amanda said, spotting a window that was slightly ajar. It was probably over the kitchen sink. If she stood on a chair she could probably get it open and climb inside. She dragged a black wrought-iron chair toward the house.

"Amanda, you are not going to break into this house," Jenny Lee said, sounding more horrified than frightened.

"I'm not going in to steal things. I just want to check things out." It was a fine distinction, but she thought a rather important one. She doubted the police would agree. Jenny Lee obviously didn't.

"And what if somebody calls the police?" Jenny Lee inquired as if she'd read her mind.

"Who would call? Take a look around, Jenny Lee. The rest of the houses on this block are still being renovated. If there are any crack dealers around, I doubt they'll be interested in calling the cops. Besides, the nearest house doesn't have a clear view over the wall."

"What about across the street? Or somebody walking past? They could hear the noise. Amanda, Oscar will have your hide if you land in jail for breaking and entering. He probably won't even bail you out."

"Oh, for heaven's sake, just hold the chair," she said, positioning it under the window. "You don't have to come in. You can go back and wait in the car, if you want to."

Jenny Lee still looked torn, but she held the chair. And as soon as Amanda got the window open and crawled inside, Jenny Lee climbed up after her and scrambled over the sill.

"If you're going to make me an accessory anyway, I might as well come along," she grumbled when Amanda shot her a questioning look.

Aside from two more empty beer bottles on the counter, the kitchen was spotless, the new white tiled counter gleaming, the cupboards tidy. The carpet in the dining room was a soft shade of Wedgwood blue, as were the walls halfway up. A white chair-rail molding all the way around the room separated the blue from the old-fashioned wallpaper on top. There was no furniture.

The sound of the music grew slightly louder as they neared the living room. There, a blend of what appeared to be a handful of family heirlooms mixed with one or two colonial reproductions. It was tasteful and cozy, if still a little barren. Wood had been laid in the fireplace awaiting the first cold evening. Several magazines were stacked neatly atop a small mahogany table. *Forbes, Fortune, Business Weekly*. No surprises there.

Amanda headed for the stairs.

"You're going up?" Jenny Lee's voice squeaked.

"Might as well."

"Oh, Lord," Jenny Lee moaned, but she followed.

The bedroom was as neatly organized as everything downstairs. Not even a pair of socks had been left on the floor. In the master bathroom, the toothpaste tube was standing upright in a cup, the top in place, no dribbles of toothpaste along the sides. There wasn't even a drip mark on the tile below the toothbrush.

"This guy must have been a neatness freak," Jenny Lee observed. "It's almost creepy."

"Maybe being compulsive is how he noticed a flaw in the bank's records," Amanda reminded her.

"I don't care. It's still weird. What are we looking for anyway?"

"Something that doesn't fit. Maybe a hiding place. If he had proof of what was going on at the bank, he probably hid it. Maybe somewhere in his house. Let's try the room across the hall. It could be an office."

Actually it was a computer hack's dream room. State-of-the-art equipment filled one end of the room. Another wall was lined with books and file cabinets. Amanda wondered if Richard Howell had used his home computer to break through the bank's security system on his own time or if he'd been high enough in the hierarchy to do his sleuthing on the job.

She dug through the trash can, which was filled with printouts, hoping to find something related to the bank. All she found were what appeared to be pages of a draft of a science fiction story. She'd never read much science fiction, but this appeared to be plausible plotting, although it was ineptly written. On closer examination, she realized that three shelves were crammed with sci-fi paperbacks.

She was about to explore the files when she heard a noise downstairs, the sound of a key turning in the lock. Jenny Lee apparently heard it, too. Her expression stricken, she waited for Amanda to come up with a way out of their predicament. Unfortunately, Amanda was much more adept at getting into trouble than getting out of it.

"Just stay very quiet until we figure out who it is."

"Maybe we should hide in the closet," Jenny Lee whispered back, moving toward the door.

Amanda reached out and put a hand on her arm.

"The door could squeak. Besides, we might not be able to hear from inside. Stay still and listen."

She figured there were two possibilities. Richard Howell was alive and coming home from a nice dinner, or his killers were breaking in to conduct a search similar to the one she and Jenny Lee were attempting. While they waited to see which, her heart was thumping at a rate only slightly slower than a drum just hitting its stride in a jazz tune.

The front door opened but didn't close. The killers, then, she guessed. They must be using the key they'd stripped from Howell's body the preceding night. She decided not to let Jenny Lee in on her suspicions quite yet. There was no telling what her reaction would be, but panic was definitely one of the options they could least afford. She held tight to Jenny Lee's hand and kept listening.

It was just as well she decided to keep silent, because among the voices she heard in the next instant, one was distinctly familiar. Amanda released a sigh that was part relief and a good bit of dismay.

"What is it?" Jenny Lee demanded in a frightened whisper.

"Let's go," Amanda said, sounding resigned.

"Go? Down there? Are you crazy?"

"We might as well. If Detective Harrison finds us hiding in the den, he's liable to shoot first and ask questions later."

Jenny Lee blinked. "That's the police down there?"

Amanda nodded.

"Oh my gosh."

"My sentiments exactly."

Amanda led the way to the top of the stairs. Midway

down she injected a cheerful note into her voice and called out, "Hi, guys. Fancy meeting you here."

Jim Harrison rounded the corner to the foyer so fast that the fancy oriental throw rug almost skidded straight into the opposite wall. When he'd regained his balance, he glared at the pair of them.

"What took you so long?" Amanda asked, seizing the conversational initiative since he seemed to be speechless with exasperation.

"Crazy me. I stopped to make it all nice and legal. I suppose you stooped to breaking and entering."

"I prefer to think of that call I got yesterday as an open invitation to drop by."

Harrison didn't seem impressed by her logic. His look of fury hadn't abated one bit. "I ought to throw you in jail for this."

"But you won't," Amanda said confidently.

"Oh? And why is that?"

"Because you know I can be helpful."

"Right now I think that's questionable."

"Face it, we think alike. Come on up here and let's to through the paperwork together. It'll save a lot of time."

Under the circumstances, Jim Harrison might have gone along with her. Amanda could tell that from the ambivalent expression that sketched across his face, then vanished when he realized there were two other police officers waiting expectantly to see what he'd do.

"Out of here!" he said at the top of his lungs. "I want you two out of here in the next ten seconds or I'll have Ralph here put handcuffs on the both of you and haul your asses downtown. You can cool your heels overnight in a cell. It'd give you a well-deserved opportunity to think about ethics and breaking the law."

Jenny Lee was scrambling down the steps before he'd concluded the threat. Amanda took her time. At the base of the steps, she started to argue her case, then caught the warning look in his eyes. His threat might have been mostly for show, but he wouldn't hesitate to act on it, if she tested him in front of subordinates.

"I'll be in the office, if you come up with anything," she said.

"I'll keep that in mind," he said dryly.

"By the way, Howell worked at the National Bank of the Netherlands," she said, tossing the detective a conciliatory crumb to show there were no hard feelings.

At the car, she found Jenny Lee leaning against the fender, trying to catch her breath. Apparently she'd run all the way from the house.

"You okay?" Amanda asked.

"Fine, now," Jenny Lee said, still sounding breathless.

When she finally looked up and met Amanda's gaze, there was a surprising, but distinct spark of excitement in her eyes. Amanda recognized that expression all too well. She felt an instant's guilt for having instilled it in Jenny Lee.

"Jenny Lee, I thought you were terrified in there."

"I was," she admitted, then grinned. "It was fantastic. Is it always like that? What are we doing next? How about the personnel files at the bank? I'll bet we could figure out a way to break in and get to those."

To Amanda's horror, she sounded serious. Feeling duty-bound to prevent Jenny Lee from getting in over her head someday, but not unaware of the irony of her telling anyone not to take chances, Amanda tried to set her straight.

"Jenny Lee, breaking and entering is a last resort. It is dangerous and illegal, especially at banks," she lectured. The proof of that was in the narrow escape they'd just had. Only Jim Harrison's benevolence had saved them from jail time. "It is not meant to pump up your adrenaline."

Jenny Lee regarded her with tolerant amusement. "Who do you think you're kidding, Amanda? That gave you a rush. You loved every dangerous second of it."

Amanda kept silent as long as she could, then grinned. "Yeah, I did."

# CHAPTER

## Six

OSCAR was pacing the reception area when Amanda and Jenny Lee stepped off the elevator a half-hour later.

"In my office," he snapped. "Now."

Amanda had the distinct impression that he wasn't pleased with them. She doubted it was because they hadn't called. In fact, if she had to hazard a guess, it would be that Jim Harrison had brought him up to date on their adventures. It would be just like the detective to figure out that Oscar's wrath would be worse than any jail sentence.

When she and Jenny Lee were seated, Oscar stood over them, puffing his cigar so hard that smoke encircled them. Amanda had a hunch the gesture was deliberate and a sure sign that exasperation had triumphed over manners.

"What the hell were you two thinking of?" he demanded finally.

"I gather you've heard from the police," Amanda said. "What about Dunne? Has he called?"

"I am not your goddamned secretary. Check your voice mail. And stop trying to change the subject. Reporters do not break and enter. At least my reporters don't. Is that clear?"

"Yes, sir," Jenny Lee said dutifully, carefully keeping her gaze averted from Amanda.

"Amanda?"

"Absolutely."

He nodded and sat down. A heavy silence fell, as he apparently pondered what to do with the two of them. Finally he ground out the cigar, which he knew damned well he wasn't supposed to be smoking in the first place, and said, "So, what'd you find?"

Amanda bit back a grin. Despite the dutiful lecture on ethics, Oscar occasionally displayed the sensibilities of a tabloid journalist who was only one step above digging for clues in celebrity garbage. If he was aware of the dichotomy in his behavior, he'd never acknowledge it.

"Nothing concrete," she said. "No sign of Howell. I couldn't even find a snapshot to prove he was the guy in the cemetery. The den was outfitted with the latest computer equipment. It's possible he's a hacker."

"You think that's how he got his information?"

"Maybe that. Maybe from the inside. There's no way to tell. We didn't have time to sort through his papers for any sort of bank documents or to look for a hiding place where he might have stashed them for safekeeping. The big advantage we have for now is that the police don't know what they're looking for in there and we do. I could go back in the morning for a more thorough check.''

Oscar groaned. "Amanda, didn't you hear a word I said a minute ago?''

''Yes.''

''Then stop telling me you plan to do the same damned thing again tomorrow.''

She grinned at the careful phrasing. "Right. I'll keep my plans to myself, so you'll be pure and innocent when anyone asks. Just remember you told me to do that the next time you're ready to blow your stack because you can't find me. If he forgets, Jenny Lee, I want you to remind him.''

He scowled at her. "I don't want to hear this. I'm going home. What about you two?''

Amanda glanced at Jenny Lee. "Why don't you go on home? There's nothing more we can do tonight.''

''Are you leaving, too?'' Jenny Lee asked, clearly unwilling to be left out of any further action Amanda planned for the night. Her adrenaline was probably still in overdrive.

''I'm going to go through that data base again, see if there's anything else that might tie in with what little we know.''

''I could help,'' Jenny Lee offered.

Amanda shook her head. "You go on. When you see Larry, tell him to set aside some time to take pictures at the cemetery, at Howell's house, and maybe an exterior shot of the bank. We might as well have photos ready to go when we finally crack this story.''

''You need him tomorrow?''

''Or the next day,'' Amanda said. "Tell him to check in with us tomorrow.''

When Oscar and Jenny Lee were gone, Amanda

called her mother to let her know it would be at least another hour or two until she got home. "Are you finding everything you need?"

"I'm fine, dear. I heated up some soup. You really could use some groceries."

Amanda knew that was a massive understatement. The only thing she kept on hand in quantity was her supply of gourmet jelly beans. "We can shop tomorrow," she promised. "Everything else okay?"

"Fine. I think I'll read a while and go on to bed. I'll see you in the morning."

The fact that her mother was ready to crawl back into bed again when it was barely nine o'clock gave Amanda yet another indication of just how depressed she was. Normally she survived on a few hours of sleep a night, hating to waste time asleep when she could be doing things—gardening, lunching at the country club, attending civic meetings, planning fund-raisers, reading. She was a voracious reader, everything from sexy potboilers to nonfiction exposés of mafia life or the intricacies of the latest banking or business scandals. She took all of the New York newspapers and rarely finished perusing them before her daily lunch at the country club.

As she thought of all that reading, Amanda realized she ought to tell her mother about this investigation. Who knew what she might have stumbled across in those newspapers and magazines that would be helpful.

Amanda thought of the sad, lost look in her mother's eyes and made up her mind that something had to be done to put a spark back in them again. Filled with a sense of purpose and determination, she picked up the phone and dialed.

The minute she heard the phone ringing in New York, though, Amanda regretted placing the call. She was exhausted and irritated, no state in which to try to reason with her father, who tended to be difficult when he felt under attack. Just as she was about to hang up, however, he answered.

She'd hoped to find him sounding every bit as depressed and lonely as her mother, but he sounded more cheerful than he had in decades. There was music in the background. Oldies from the '50's, if she wasn't mistaken. Apparently he was reliving years gone by.

"Dad?"

"Oh, hi, pumpkin. What are you doing calling at this hour?" He cut the volume on the stereo, though not so low that she couldn't hear a few final strains of "Don't Be Cruel."

It was nine at night, not three in the morning, she thought grumpily. His perfectly reasonable tone made her want to hop on the next flight to New York and whap him over the head with one of his outrageously expensive golf clubs. Were all men this blind to the wake of emotional chaos they left behind or was it only the ones she knew?

"Dad, you know perfectly well why I'm calling."

There was a beat of silence, except for some appropriately mournful ballad by Johnny Mathis, who'd replaced Elvis. Then he said, "I guess you've heard from your mother."

"Heard from her," she repeated incredulously, her voice climbing as she succumbed to indignation. "She's your wife. Don't you even know where she is?"

"She told me she was going to a hotel," he said, sounding defensive. "I offered to leave, but she insisted."

The last of Amanda's fragile thread of patience snapped. "Hotel, hell. She is sitting in my living room in Georgia, crying her eyes out last time I checked."

Actually her mother had been distressingly calm when she called, but a little guilt heaped on her father wouldn't hurt. Even though her mother had yet to spill any details, chances were extremely good that he deserved it.

"I see," he said.

"Do you? Do you really? Well, I don't see a damned thing. I wish someone would explain it to me."

"Amanda, calm down. Yelling won't solve anything."

"Calm down? It wasn't bad enough that my own relationship blew up in my face, now my parents have both taken leave of their senses? Dad, what the hell is going on? Are you having a fling with some twenty-year-old bimbo?"

The appalled gasp told her she'd gone too far.

"Amanda Jane Bailey Roberts," he said in a furious tone she'd rarely heard despite a long string of adolescent transgressions. "I will not allow you to use that disrespectful tone with me. I am still your father. I am not one of your news sources you need to bully for information. Call me back when you want to discuss this rationally."

Before she could say another word, he hung up, quietly, but with absolute finality.

Amanda stared at the phone. Well, she'd certainly handled that well. Why couldn't she have used the same reasonable tone as her father? Maybe then she'd have answers, instead of a knot in her stomach and more questions.

As if in response to her plaintive thought, the phone rang. She snatched it up, hoping it was her slow-to-anger, quick-to-forgive father, ready to make amends to her, if not to her mother.

"Working late, aren't you?" said FBI Special Agent Jeffrey Dunne.

Her spirits plummeted. "Oh, it's you."

"Somehow I'd hoped for a warmer response."

"You're lucky I don't fire a cannon straight into the receiver. You have a lot of nerve calling here, Agent Dunne."

"You called me. Remember? And for a woman trying to get a handle on a banking scandal, you're being awfully testy with a prospective source."

Amanda drew in a deep breath and tried to get a grip on her ragged emotions. Maybe it would help her to figure out how he knew what story she was working on. "How do you know what I'm investigating?" she asked suspiciously. "Are you spying on me again?"

"Ouch," he said, though he didn't seem to take offense. A thick hide came with the turf, no doubt. "Do you want help with this or not? I assumed that was why you called."

"I'm supposed to cling to some wild idea that you intend to share information with me?" Though she had called with exactly that wild hope, she added sarcastically, "You'll pardon me if I put my money on flying pigs."

"Care to go for coffee and take your chances?"

Amanda considered the invitation. Jeffrey Dunne had been at the heart of the plot to use Donelli as a lure to get her to shake things up among the Klan members and skinheads still lurking in the Georgia shadows. He was a sneaky, underhanded, devious creep of the first order. He was also, however, an agent of the federal agency that might know what the hell was going on with Richard Howell's bank. Given her present mood, it was a tough call.

"Where?" she asked finally.

"I'll pick you up downstairs in fifteen minutes."

"I'd rather crawl fifty miles than get in a car with a slime like you," she said to save face after caving in so quickly. "Just tell me where to meet you."

One of Jeffrey Dunne's few saving graces was his sense of humor. He laughed and named an all-night diner nearby.

"I'll be looking forward to it," he added.

To Amanda's astonishment, he sounded as if he meant it. Her suspicious nature went on full alert. The last time Agent Dunne had been that friendly, he'd put her on an emotional roller-coaster to hell.

With his short-cropped brown hair and standard issue gray suit, he looked innocent enough as he watched the door of the diner. He'd chosen an isolated booth against a far wall, probably so that others who felt as Amanda did about him couldn't get a clear shot at his back. He stood as she approached, his expression solemn, although Amanda thought she detected a smile trying to sneak free from all his determined stoicism.

"You look good, Amanda."

She ignored the compliment, despite the obvious sincerity and good manners with which it had been spoken. "What do you have for me?"

"Coffee. Black," he said, gesturing toward the cup on the table.

She scowled at the deliberate evasion. "I can still leave."

"But you won't, as long as there's a chance in hell that I might know something you want to know."

"Do you?"

"I'll tell you the answer to that if you'll ease up on the tough-reporter routine."

"Why should I do that? I am a tough reporter."

"I know, but I think I liked the vulnerability I saw during that last case better."

"I'm sure you did. It was convenient as hell for you, wasn't it?"

He grinned. "All right. Now we're getting down to it, aren't we? We probably should have had this conversation months ago and put the entire incident behind us. You're still mad as hell at me for not telling you the truth about Joe and what happened on your wedding day."

"I'm mad as hell at Donelli," she corrected. "As for you, I give you about as much thought as pond scum."

He nodded soberly, but there was a disturbing twinkle in his eyes. It appeared that Agent Dunne didn't take her seriously. Of course, he never had. If he'd given a damn about her or her feelings, he would never have played her for a fool the way he had. Of course, since he represented the Federal Bureau of Investigation, he had the official right to jerk average citizens around. A few choruses of the national anthem played in her head, underscoring the thought.

She studied Jeffrey Dunne intently as if that might help her ascertain exactly why he'd responded so readily to her call tonight. Although he'd obviously guessed what she wanted and claimed to have relevant information, she had a sneaking suspicion that he planned to use her again. How he planned to do that was yet to be determined. It would be absolutely fascinating to watch him try.

"I hear you told the Atlanta police that you witnessed a murder the other night," he said after several minutes of speculative silence.

"I didn't think you and Jim Harrison kept up with each other," she commented dryly. More accurately, as she recalled, they hated each other's guts. Too many jurisdictional disputes and not enough professional respect.

"Actually you brought us together," he retorted cheerfully. "Gave us something in common."

"Oh?"

"Yes. We both find you worrisome."

"Must mean I'm doing my job."

"So, tell me about this murder you think you saw."

"There is no question about what I saw, Special Agent Dunne."

"It used to be 'Jeffrey.' "

"That was when I trusted you."

For an instant Amanda could have sworn she saw a hint of sorrow in his steady, brown eyes.

"Okay," he said eventually. "Let's keep this businesslike for the moment. You were meeting a source. A bullet silenced him in the middle of his divulging his secrets and then the body vanished."

"Why'd you need me? You have the story down cold."

"I was hoping for all the juicy details as only you can assemble them."

"Why? This is just some run-of-the-mill local murder, isn't it?" she said innocently. "In fact, Atlanta PD won't even go that far unless they can come up with a victim. I'm sure it has nothing to do with the FBI." She paused, wide-eyed with expectation. "Or am I wrong about that?"

"Okay, Amanda, let's stop fencing. Obviously you know or suspect that something more is going on here. What did you hear and from whom?"

"Why the hell should I tell you?"

"Because it's a fair exchange for the information you hope to get from me."

"Then you go first. I figure you owe me that much at least. Is there or is there not a federal investigation of activities at a certain bank here in town?"

"Not exactly," he hedged.

"No?" she said skeptically. "Come on."

"Amanda, would it do any good at all for me to warn you away from this? It's not what it seems. I swear to you."

"Then what is it?"

"I can't tell you that, because I honestly don't know."

She regarded him incredulously. "Just a simple messenger, then? That must gall you. Frankly, I doubt it anyway. You can't honestly expect me to thank you politely for the rather innocuous warning and bow out of this investigation, can you?"

"Expect, no," he said ruefully. "I can always hope. It would make both our lives a helluva lot easier."

"Sorry. No can do. You've just increased my curiosity tenfold."

He winced. "I was afraid of that. Let me give you a bit of friendly advice then. Lay low. For once in your adventurous life you are in way over your head. Take my word for it."

"Your word?" she repeated. "You've already admitted you don't know what the hell is happening. Besides, don't you get it? I wouldn't take your word that the sky is blue."

He shook his head. "Dammit, I knew they should have sent somebody else to have this conversation with you. Amanda, whatever's going on here—and like I said I'll be damned if I know myself exactly what it is—you don't want to get mixed up in it. People at some very high levels are keeping a close watch on this situation. They don't want it splashed all over the media."

"What *situation?*"

"I can't say. It's a matter of national security."

"And that's supposed to deter me? You should know better. Now I want to know how high this watchdog is. Director of the FBI? Secretary of State, maybe? How about President?"

"I said it involved national security, dammit."

"I want someone higher than you to tell me that. Then I'll back off. Otherwise you're wasting this marvelous display of intimidation."

This time there was no doubt about the alarm and the genuine concern in his eyes. The alarm didn't worry her much. However, she had to admit she found that concern . . . disconcerting. Troubling.

Actually, she found it a damned nuisance. If she bought into it, she might have to take a step back and reexamine exactly what she might be getting into with this investigation and whose toes she might be stepping on. If not the FBI's, and that was Dunne's implication, then whose? And exactly how miserable were they likely to make her life before she got to the truth? Normally a few good punches would never get her down, but lately she was already on the ropes. A few good punches might knock her down for the count.

She stood up slowly and dropped a dollar on the table for the coffee. "Thanks for the advice."

He tried to hand her money back to her. "The coffee's on me, too."

Amanda shook her head. "If I'm not planning to heed your advice, I can hardly accept your coffee. See you around."

She heard his mumbled expletive as he scrambled

from the booth to follow her, but a waitress who'd been stiffed by customers one time too many blocked his way just long enough to allow Amanda to make her escape. He got to the door just as she drove past the restaurant at a clip slightly in excess of the legal limit. Tempting fate again, Donelli would say.

She waved.

Agent Dunne did not.

Yes, indeed, she was definitely tempting fate.

# CHAPTER

## *Seven*

AMANDA was still trying to figure out what to make of her enigmatic conversation with Jeffrey Dunne when she drove her mother to Virginia's bakery for breakfast the following morning. They had gone no more than a mile when she caught her mother's bemused expression as she stared out the window at the countryside. Apparently the desolation she'd missed the day before was actually sinking in.

"Darling, where is the town?"

"This is it," Amanda replied. "A post office, a real estate office, a Seven-Eleven, and Virginia's. Oh, and the town hall, of course. We have three new parking meters out front. Did you notice?"

"You're kidding me, right?"

"No, Mother. I can almost guarantee that the nearest

Bloomingdale's is not within walking distance. Not even a Saks.''

Her mother looked stunned, though no more so than Amanda had for the entire first year she lived here. Now she'd almost gotten used to the peace and quiet, to the lazy rhythm of life in the country. Maybe that was why she didn't pay much attention to the hush that fell when they walked through the bakery doorway.

That sudden silence should definitely have been a warning. The old geezers sitting at the counter and shooting the breeze over coffee and the morning paper normally couldn't be quieted by anything less dramatic than an Atlanta Braves loss in the tenth inning or the demise of a Falcons' lead on a Sunday afternoon.

Amanda waved at Virginia Beatty, who glanced nervously toward the back of the restaurant. Her overly friendly smile as she hustled out from behind the counter had about as much sincerity as a politician's leading up to election day.

"Amanda, honey, it sure is a surprise to see you in here at this hour on a weekday morning. You're usually halfway to Atlanta by now," Virginia drawled loudly and distinctly enough to have been heard by everyone in the next county. Amanda guessed that her real target was much closer, and she had a feeling of dread that she knew exactly who it was.

Her announcement made, Virginia poured two cups of coffee and stared curiously at Amanda's mother. Then she set the pot on the Formica-topped table and pulled a pencil out of her beehive hairdo—it was an unrelenting shade of coal black this week, a slight improvement over last month's orange. Virginia's hair-coloring experiments rarely turned out well.

She nabbed an order pad out of her pocket. "Now then, ladies, what'll it be for you?"

"Mother, Virginia makes wonderful blueberry pancakes. Light and fluffy, just the way you like them. Or how about French toast?"

"Whatever, dear," her mother responded without bothering to examine the laminated menu that had been typewritten a dozen years earlier and never once altered. Doughnuts, eggs, bacon, country ham, and grits were the staples. Pancakes and sugary French toast were available for folks who wanted something more exotic. Anyone who wanted anything fancier went someplace else. Few did. Virginia served up the county's hottest gossip along with breakfast.

"I'm not really hungry," Amanda's mother said, tucking the menu back between the old-fashioned glass sugar dispenser and the salt and pepper shakers. There was no sugar substitute at Virginia's, just as there was little talk of lowering cholesterol, though she would replace butter with diet margarine if anyone asked. No one did.

Always sympathetic and sensing a juicy story to serve with lunch, Virginia looked as if she were all set to sit down and offer a little consolation to the distressed newcomer. Amanda stopped her by placing two orders for pancakes, two large glasses of orange juice, and one order of country ham.

"Uh-oh," Virginia said knowingly. She knew how Amanda's appetite blossomed during times of crisis. "I'll hurry this right up."

"No rush, dear," Mrs. Bailey told her as she absentmindedly stirred her black coffee.

"Hurry," Amanda countered.

Virginia hesitated, then leaned down to whisper,

"Amanda, honey, there's something you probably should know." She glanced pointedly toward the back booth.

Amanda could think of only one reason Virginia would be acting like the cat that swallowed the canary. Donelli. It would certainly explain the deafening silence that had fallen the minute she walked in and Virginia's high-decibel greeting.

"Joe?" she asked, and tried to identify the feeling that sparked inside. Much as she wanted to, she couldn't describe it as indifference. Not yet, dammit.

Virginia nodded. "He's been coming in quite a lot lately, ever since . . ." She faltered in a rare and futile attempt at diplomacy. "Well, you know. I guess he's been lonely out at that big old house of his. Probably hates eating breakfast alone."

"Don't you start," Amanda warned, since she already knew where Virginia's sympathies lay. Virginia had known Donelli longer and thought he was the cutest thing since Clint Black hit the country music world.

"You know perfectly well he used to come in here and gossip almost every day," Amanda reminded her. "Just like everyone else in town. His presence here is nothing new."

"If you say so," Virginia said. "Anyway, I just thought you ought to know."

"Thanks. I appreciate that."

Looking a little disappointed that Amanda hadn't reacted by throwing a plate the length of the restaurant, Virginia left her to ponder exactly how she intended to behave when Donelli eventually stood up and made his way past her table.

And he would do that. No question about it. Whoever was sitting across from him in that booth had no doubt informed him the instant she walked through the door, with Virginia's bellowed greeting to confirm the arrival. It was the sort of news people in this town just loved to deliver so they could see what sort of drama it precipitated. As Amanda could personally attest, watching crops grow wasn't nearly as fascinating.

"Joseph is here?" her mother asked when Virginia had gone back behind the counter.

"So, I'm told," Amanda said in the most nonchalant voice she could manage.

The distracted look vanished from her mother's face as she reached across and sympathetically patted Amanda's hand. "I'm so sorry, dear. I've been so wrapped up in my own problems, I haven't given a thought to yours. How do you feel about being here with that man?"

She said it as if Donelli were a condemned serial killer. Perversely, Amanda found herself wanting to leap to his defense. Thank goodness her mother prevented that by asking, "Would you rather leave? You haven't said a word about him since you called off the wedding. Your father and I haven't wanted to pry."

"There's nothing to say," Amanda said tersely, grateful now for the self-absorption that had kept her parents from asking too many questions. She wanted to keep it that way. "Could we change the subject? Did you sleep well last night?"

Her mother refused to be distracted. "Amanda? Do you want to go? If your father walked through that door right now, I know how I'd feel."

Amanda saw her opening and seized it. "Why don't we talk about that? How do you feel about Dad right now?"

"Don't try to change the subject."

"Mother, you're stonewalling me and I don't like it," Amanda said, realizing that her parents were actually quite a bit better at it than most of the government officials she questioned.

"Yes, I am," her mother agreed pointedly. "Now, do you want to leave or not?"

Amanda sighed and conceded that for the moment she was not going to get a straight answer about her parents' marital problems. "No, I do not want to leave. I'm not going to run away whenever we bump into each other. In a community this small, I'd have to spend all my time hiding at home."

Her mother gave her a wry look. "That sounds very mature, dear. Now tell me how you really feel."

"If it wouldn't cause a scene and I weren't starved, I'd be out the door," she replied honestly. Hurt had nudged aside anger over the past few weeks, a transition she deeply regretted at the moment. The desire to stab him with one of the dull knives on the table might have been preferable to the sinking sensation in the pit of her stomach. She met her mother's concerned gaze evenly, just as Joe stood up, then shrugged. "Too late now."

She could tell from Donelli's expression that he'd gotten all the hints about her presence, probably knew every detail about her appearance down to what she was wearing. If he was ill-at-ease, it didn't show. He threw a couple of dollars onto his table and strolled down the narrow aisle until he reached her, then paused. He jammed his hands into the back pockets of his jeans, leaned back on his heels, and surveyed her with that lazy, careful look that missed nothing. He nodded politely.

"Amanda."

She glanced up, then away. "Hello."

"You look good."

"Thank you." She dared to meet his gaze. Despite his outward appearance of calm and good manners, there was turmoil in the depths of his eyes. He had never wanted this separation. She had demanded it. "How are you?"

"Good. Taking things easy now that all the crops are in." He glanced at her mother, his expression curious, then slowly changing to genuine pleasure as recognition dawned. He'd seen her picture on Amanda's dresser, and despite her mother's wan complexion there was no mistaking her classic looks. At her best Elisa Hunt Bailey was reminiscent of old photos of Lauren Bacall with that sweeping, provocative wave of chestnut hair. She'd even taken the time for makeup this morning. She had an expert's touch at concealment.

Amanda couldn't see any way around making the introduction. "Mother, this is Joe Donelli. Joe, my mother."

He took her hand and held it. "Mrs. Bailey, you have . . ." His eyes focused on Amanda. "You have a wonderful daughter. I'm very sorry that I hurt her."

The words were spoken to Mrs. Bailey but it was clear that the apology was meant for Amanda, a reminder that even though he'd felt certain he'd done the only thing he could by joining forces with the FBI, he was genuinely sorry for causing her pain.

"So am I," Mrs. Bailey said bluntly.

Donelli grinned. "I see how you developed that tendency not to pull punches," he said to Amanda. "Mrs. Bailey, I'm sorry it took so long for us to meet. I hope you enjoy your visit." Again his gaze lingered on Amanda. Finally he said, "Amanda," then nodded and left.

A collective sigh seemed to ease out around the

bakery. There was a sudden rustling of newspapers as everyone tried to pretend they hadn't been eavesdropping on every word spoken by the estranged couple. By nightfall they'd probably be taking bets on a reconciliation.

Donelli had no sooner walked away than Amanda started telling her mother every last detail of the investigation she'd just started. If she talked fast enough, perhaps her mother wouldn't plague her with more questions about Donelli. The beginnings of a concerned protest eventually died on her mother's lips as Amanda trotted out every fascinating tidbit she'd scraped up thus far.

"So what do you think?" she asked finally.

Her mother regarded her in astonishment. "You're asking me?" she said as if Amanda had never sought her opinion before.

"You read all those books on the BCCI scandal. You told me so. You probably know more about shady banking in this country than I do."

A pleased expression crossed her mother's face, before she turned thoughtful. Amanda waited, lost in her memories of the man who'd just walked away. A few months ago she would have been having this conversation with him. Resentment and regret settled in in equal proportions.

"You think this involves arms," her mother said eventually between absentminded bites of her pancakes. "Guns or technology?"

Amanda dragged her attention back to the story. "I don't know. The source didn't specify."

"My guess would be military technology," her mother said.

For the first time since her arrival, a faint spark of excitement blossomed in her eyes. Amanda could see that, like Dorothy Gilman's Mrs. Pollifax, Elisa Hunt Bailey would probably leap at the chance to be a spy. The revelation surprised her.

Then again, how much did she really know about her mother's dreams, about what she might have been if she'd chosen to be something other than Mrs. Nelson Bailey? *Almost nothing,* she was forced to admit.

Caught up in the speculation, she told Amanda, "Dual-use technology is easier to slip past the regulators, you know. A third country could buy the technology under the guise of using it for nonmilitary purposes, then turn around and sell it to Iraq. Do any Georgia companies manufacture that sort of thing?"

Impressed by her mother's quick grasp of the complexities of the case, Amanda drew a notebook out of her purse and began jotting notes. "I'm not sure, but I'll check it out today. Okay, what else?"

Her mother shot her another pleased smile. "Any local arms merchants?"

"None that I'm aware of," she said, enjoying her mother's obvious enthusiasm. "I wonder if I could track down some questionable characters in that particular underworld by using those soldier-of-fortune magazines."

"I thought you had sources with the police and FBI," her mother said.

"They're not especially happy with me at the moment. I think I'd better not count on official help." She regarded her mother with renewed amazement. "You know, I expected you to pitch a fit when you heard about all this. Instead, you suddenly seem energized."

Her mother shrugged. "I suppose for me it's a much-needed distraction. And it's theoretical. For you, I don't know. You tend to rush in with all these high ideals. You never wanted to be Lois Lane. You wanted to be Superman. That terrified me from my nice, safe, suburban perspective. All this clandestine business promises a good bit of danger."

Amanda waited for the rest of the lecture. Instead, her mother said, "But you're a grown woman, Amanda. You have to do what makes you happy. I've finally accepted that."

"Tracking down the bad guys does give me a sense of satisfaction," Amanda said. "I feel as if I'm making a difference."

"I wish I felt that way about my life," her mother said wistfully. "Sometimes I wish I'd chosen a career like this. Then maybe this business with your father wouldn't have thrown me so." She sighed, a look of reflection in her eyes. "Ah, well, too late now. I can always live vicariously through you."

For one fleeting instant Amanda considered asking her mother to work with her on this story. But that would be a disaster. She was so busy trying to squelch the idea that she didn't notice the sudden excitement in her mother's expression.

"Darling, I have a wonderful idea," she said. "Why don't I help you out?"

"Why don't you what?" Amanda replied in measured tones, trying to keep the horror out of her voice.

"Help out. I'm sure you can use an assistant. You wouldn't have to pay me. Just think what fun it would be, the two of us working together."

*Fun* was not the word that popped into Amanda's head.

"Mother, it's really thoughtful of you to volunteer, but Jenny Lee is really counting on being my assistant. She's earned the chance."

"This needn't change that. Surely there's enough work for two."

Amanda felt as if she were being smothered. However, she couldn't come up with a single, rational argument to stop her mother from plunging into this project. Every excuse she managed sounded selfish, maybe even a little hysterical. Of course, she felt a little hysterical. Working with her mother. Dear Lord.

Still, she couldn't kill that first sign of enthusiasm she'd seen in her mother's eyes since she'd arrived from New York. No doubt her mother was grasping at straws these days too.

"I suppose Jenny Lee could try to get a job at the bank," Amanda said reluctantly. "She's so innocent and naïve, they'll never suspect her of snooping. If that works out, I would need someone else to help with research."

"There, you see. It's perfect." Her delight faltered. "Are you sure you're not just agreeing to this to keep me entertained?"

That was exactly what she was doing but she couldn't bring herself to say so. "Mother, if you find this entertaining, all the better. It will be wonderful to have somebody to share the workload."

"What about your boss, though? What will he have to say about it?"

Amanda knew exactly what Oscar would say. But once he'd cooled down, he would see the value in having an extra resource on the investigative team. They'd be that much likelier to get the story before anyone else and in time for the next edition of the magazine.

"He'll be thrilled," she said, stretching the truth like Spandex over a fat woman's rear.

# CHAPTER

## *Eight*

O scar wasn't thrilled. However, he managed to be polite given Elisa Bailey's presence in the doorway of his office. Despite her own misgivings about this scheme, Amanda hadn't counted on him to bail her out anyway. She knew he was constitutionally incapable of insulting anyone's mother, even hers.

"Welcome aboard," he said through gritted teeth.

"Thank you. I'll do my best to be helpful," Amanda's mother replied, regarding him as if he were a foreign species she'd never seen before. The men in Elisa Hunt Bailey's circles did not look as if they'd bought their clothes at a K mart sale and put them on straight out of a dryer.

"Well, we'd better get to work then," Amanda said, grabbing her mother by the wrist before she could suggest a dry-cleaner. She was heading back to the newsroom when Oscar stopped her in her tracks.

"Amanda!" Oscar said. The quiet tone belied the unspoken command. "Perhaps we could talk a few minutes." He smiled at her mother as if to reassure her that any sting in his voice was harmless. Amanda knew better.

"Darling, why don't I go to the library and get some of those books we talked about earlier," her mother offered. "They'll refresh my memory."

Oscar looked as if he were about to explode. Amanda rushed through directions to the library and sent her mother on her way. The minute the door was closed behind her, Oscar snapped, "What the hell were you thinking of?"

"Excuse me?"

"She's your mother. She's not a journalist. Has she ever done anything like this before? If you wanted a research assistant, you should have asked. What was I supposed to say with her standing right here?"

"Exactly what you did say," Amanda told him. "Thank you. You have no idea how grateful I am. This is just what she needs."

"Amanda, this isn't some halfway house for people at loose ends. What about what I need? What about what this magazine needs? Did you think for a minute about that?"

"Of course I did," she snapped, irritated that she had to defend a decision that hadn't been hers in the first place. "She'll do a good job. She knows her way around a library. She's smart. She knows a helluva lot more about banking than I do."

"Then maybe I should just turn the whole damned

story over to her. Where am I supposed to get the money to pay her?''

''She's not looking for a paycheck. If it comes to that, I'll pay her. The money's not important. She needs a boost to her self-esteem. I need help. It's as simple as that.''

Oscar shook his head. ''You never cease to amaze me.''

Amanda managed a halfhearted grin. ''That's certainly always been my goal in life.''

''And Jenny Lee? I thought you were championing her career this week?''

''What would you think of putting her inside the bank?''

''Jesus, Amanda, why not ask for the moon? I'm supposed to send her off on assignment and call in a temp for that job, too? Do you have any other plans for this magazine I ought to know about?''

Amanda decided that now was not the time to tell him about the new hot-trend section she'd been tossing around in her mind over the past few weeks. ''Think of it this way. If the bank pays well enough, Jenny Lee will probably let you give her regular salary to the temp.''

''If it pays that well, she'll probably stay on and then where will we be?'' he shot right back, then sighed with resignation. ''Fine. Send her. What makes you think she can get the job?''

''She worked her way through college as a teller in her daddy's bank. That's just one of those little facts you'd know if you ever read the damned résumés you make us fill out.''

Before sending Jenny Lee off to infiltrate the bank, Amanda decided to pay a call on the manager. She wanted a better fix on Richard Howell's role at the bank. She also wanted to assure herself that the undercover attempt wouldn't put the sometimes impetuous, aspiring reporter in any immediate danger. And it wouldn't hurt to take a firsthand look at what was most likely the scene of the alleged crime.

The National Bank of the Netherlands was near Peachtree Center, only a few stops away on the MARTA. Amanda didn't bother to sit down as the train whooshed through the underground tunnel. The escalator to ground level was stalled. By the time she'd hiked the endless stairs, she was panting. Another one or two reminders like this and she might actually have to take up jogging. Her last experience with aerobics hadn't turned out so well. The instructor had been murdered. Amanda had flunked the class, but she had found the killer. She figured she'd gotten the best of the deal.

Checking her reflection in the tinted glass of the highrise bank building, she straightened the scarf she'd knotted around her neck that morning in an attempt to dress up her usual slacks, T-shirt, and blazer for her mother's sake. Under normal conditions, Elisa Hunt Bailey would wear pearls to a garage sale. Even today, she'd rallied and worn a snazzy silk pants and jacket ensemble that was probably considered casual among her stylish friends.

Inside the impressive bank lobby, thick rose carpeting edged a wide sweep of gray marble. The rosewood furniture looked as if it had been taken straight off the showroom floor of the most contemporary Scandinavian designer. The hushed atmosphere suggested that important business involving huge amounts of money was taking place here. There were no snaking lines of people nudged into order by velvet ropes and metal stanchions. At first glance, in fact, it appeared that there were more employees than customers. Given the way she felt about standing in bank lines, Amanda was tempted to transfer her checking account on the spot.

Instead, she made her way across the lobby to a doorway discreetly marked *executive offices*. A guard— not a receptionist, but an armed guard—sat at the desk to bar the common folk from straying inside.

"Yes, miss?" he said cheerfully enough. If you ignored the gun, he looked like a cherubic grandfather.

"I was hoping to see the manager," she said.

"You have an appointment?"

"No."

"Sorry. Ms. Van Sant doesn't see anyone without an appointment. Those are the rules."

"Maybe you can help. Did you know a young man who worked here by the name of Richard Howell?"

The man's expression suddenly lost some of its friendliness. His gaze turned downright frosty, in fact. "Who'd you say you are?"

"Amanda Roberts. I had a call from Mr. Howell the other day and I've been trying to reach him ever since," she improvised. "I was in the neighborhood today and thought I'd just drop by and try to catch him. Is he around?"

"No."

No elaboration, she noticed. "Then perhaps I should speak to Ms. Van Sant about him."

He considered that, then finally nodded. "I'll check."

The call to the inner sanctum took less than a minute. When he hung up, he seemed surprised by the manager's response, but he reached for the door. "You can go in. The office is at the end of the hall."

"Thanks."

A young man with a blond flattop and chiseled features sat just outside Ms. Van Sant's office. Although he was dressed in business attire, Amanda had the distinct impression that he had a gun tucked inside his tailored navy blue suit. If not, all those apparent muscles could probably be put to effective use in a crisis. His expression wasn't especially warm, but he waved her inside.

Given the security, Amanda wasn't sure what to expect of Ms. Van Sant. The elegant woman who stepped from behind the rosewood desk wore her frosted hair pulled neatly back from a porcelain complexion that cosmetic companies liked to believe their products could produce. There was a shrewd intelligence in the assessing look she directed at Amanda. If she was suspicious about Amanda's interest in Richard Howell, she had concealed it.

"I understand you were asking about one of my employees," she said.

"Yes. Richard Howell."

"I'm sorry but he isn't in. He hasn't been in for several days," she said, sounding miffed. "Actually, when the guard said you'd mentioned his name, I was hoping you'd come to explain his whereabouts."

"Sorry," Amanda said. "It is a mystery to me. Has he done anything like this before?"

Ms. Van Sant looked horrified by the very notion. "Absolutely not. I do not tolerate this sort of behavior. When he eventually turns up, he will be here only long enough to be terminated. I expect my employees to be responsible. That does not include taking off without a word to anyone."

Amanda noticed that the banker was more annoyed

than concerned. If she was feeling the slightest bit guilty, it was hidden well by the exasperation. "But do you know for sure that he isn't sick or on vacation?" Amanda asked.

"I haven't the faintest idea where he is or what he's doing." She sounded like a woman to whom that rarely happened.

"I see. Does he hold a particularly important position?"

"We operate with great efficiency here. All of our employees are critical. If you're asking if he was an executive, the answer is no. He was in one of our management training groups. Fortunately, such positions are easily filled these days, given the number of banks tightening their operations."

Amanda had a feeling Richard Howell's position would be filled by the end of the day if Jenny Lee hauled herself down here in a hurry. She debated leaving a business card, but decided she didn't want Ms. Van Sant knowing just yet that she was a reporter. "Do you mind if I check back in a day or two to see if you've heard from him?"

"Certainly not. Just ask my secretary. I'll see to it that he knows he's to tell you what's become of him."

An interesting choice of words, Amanda thought, but she merely smiled back. "Thanks."

Back at *Inside Atlanta,* Amanda checked in with Jenny Lee. "Any sign of my mother?"

"She called once about twenty minutes ago. She said she'd call back."

"Great."

"Amanda, exactly what is your mother doing? Oscar said she's working here."

"I gave her some research to do. I can use the help, and she needs to rebuild her self-confidence."

"Oh," Jenny Lee said flatly.

Amanda caught the look of disappointment Jenny Lee was trying valiantly to hide. She perched on the edge of the receptionist's desk. "Oscar and I talked about where you could do the most good in this investigation."

The receptionist's eyes lit up. "Really?"

"We want you to apply for a job in the bank. Get inside. See if you can find any of the illegal practices Richard Howell was trying to tell us about."

Jenny Lee grabbed a notebook. "When should I go? What should I be looking for?"

Amanda had to hide a smile at her eagerness. She outlined everything she could think of that might confirm Howell's charges. "If you can get a temp in here by this afternoon, go in right away. Ms. Van Sant doesn't seem like the type who'll want to waste time in filling the position."

"What if they don't hire me?"

"Jenny Lee, you've been a teller before. Your father is your reference. How difficult can it be? Besides, you could sweet-talk your way into heaven. I have no doubt the personnel director will be thrilled at not even having to advertise."

"If there hasn't been an ad, though, how will I explain even going there to apply for a job?"

"Just tell her you've recently left another job and you're applying everywhere."

Jenny Lee beamed. "I'll call the temp agency right now. Thanks, Amanda."

"Don't thank me. Just find me the proof I need of Howell's allegations."

Amanda was heading for her desk when Jenny Lee called after her, "Amanda, it's your mother on line three."

Oscar's desk was much closer than her own and he wasn't anywhere in sight. She stepped into his office and picked up the phone once she'd found it under a pile of file folders and computer printouts.

"Darling, I'm still doing research at the library, but a few minutes ago I had a thought. Didn't you once date a reporter named Chad Keyes?" she asked, just as Oscar returned and scowled at Amanda.

"Sorry," she mouthed at him and stepped around the desk so that he could get to his chair. To her mother she said, "I went out with Chad ten years ago and *once* was the operative word. Why on earth would you suddenly think of that?"

"Because he just did a story for the network recently," she began.

"On Armand LeConte," Amanda concluded. "Mother, you're a genius." She hung up and beamed at Oscar. "I told you she'd be worth her weight in gold."

He didn't look impressed. "Why? Because she remembers something you did ten years ago?"

"It's not what I did. It's with whom I did it."

Oscar blushed to the remaining roots of his hair. "I don't need to hear this."

"Oh, don't be such a prude. You should know the name, Oscar. Chad Keyes. He is going to get me to the most notorious arms dealer in the entire world."

# CHAPTER
## Nine

A MANDA rarely called in favors, but her mother was right. Chad Keyes could save her hours of work in tracking down the man known the world over for his suspect arms deals. Although their social relationship hadn't progressed beyond that one very casual, cautious date, Chad continued to be her most reliable network news contact. In the manner of many otherwise fiercely competitive journalists, they occasionally shared information and resources . . . as long as it didn't jeopardize their own breaking stories.

In recent years Chad had spent months on end trying to catch Armand LeConte in a slip-up. It had become an obsession. He had tried to nail the arms merchant in a rare one-on-one on-air interview that had been picked up by CNN and shown around the globe. He had failed.

The arms dealer was as cool and smooth as damp tile and twice as slippery.

Armand LeConte. The very name summoned up intrigue in news circles. He was the elusive quarry, every bit as impossible to trap as a wily fox. The debonair French expatriate, who resided on a farm in rural Virginia an hour's drive west of Washington, staunchly maintained that he was apolitical, that he was a mere merchant filling a need in the international marketplace. His contacts on Capitol Hill were neighbors and acquaintances. If they occasionally greased the wheels of the tedious bureaucratic process for him, well, wasn't that what friends were for?

He claimed all this with such self-effacing charm that entire governments had either been taken in or had given up trying to prove the flurry of charges that periodically were mounted against him. If an illegal arms deal was happening in Atlanta, Amanda was certain that LeConte would be familiar with the details, even if he wasn't involved personally. Very little in that particular subculture escaped his notice.

But first she had to reach him, and Chad Keyes could point her in the right direction. The only problem was that he would want to know why she was after LeConte, and this was one of those times when Amanda wasn't sure she was ready to share that information with the competition.

Her only reasonable alternative, however, would be to risk Jeffrey Dunne's wrath by asking him. The FBI probably had the arms dealer's address, his phone number, the names of all his dependents, and the number of gray hairs in his full head of wavy black hair. Indeed, asking Dunne would be the quickest, most direct way to go about it. It would also obligate her to the man, and that was unacceptable.

She flipped through her Rolodex and dialed Chad Keyes in Washington. Despite his preppie name and well-heeled background, Chad was a rough-and-tumble journalist with one of the sharpest minds in the business. He had an extensive wardrobe of khaki and always had a bag packed, ready to take off at the first hint of trouble anywhere in the world. His ambition and his determination to be first on any news scene topped even hers. On that first and only date, as they had traded credentials, she had recognized that they would spend far too much of their time in friendly and maybe not so friendly competition. That awareness on both their parts had stood squarely between them and any future that might have developed. They'd agreed they were best suited to friendship.

Spotting the flaws that would preclude any serious relationship had not made Amanda admire Chad any less as a journalist. He could link two threads of a story and tie the condemning knot before his competitors caught on that the story had more than one angle. That skill promised to make for a challenging conversation.

"Amanda Roberts, a voice from the past," he said in that low, smooth-as-whiskey delivery that was made to rumble over airwaves. It had been seductive at pillow talk as well, if his string of well-publicized conquests was anything to judge by. "Where the hell have you been? I thought you dropped off the face of the earth."

"Not quite so far. I landed in Georgia."

"Good Lord," he said with sympathy of someone who considered world capitals the only places worthy of his presence. "How? Why?"

"A long story for another time."

"Still married to that boring professor?"

She had forgotten that he had lodged a friendly but

vehement protest when she'd chosen to marry Mack Roberts. He was the only one who had. Everyone else had thought that Mack would bring stability into her otherwise tumultuous life. Chad had told her that living with Mack would make her lose her edge. Maybe it was just as well the marriage hadn't lasted long enough for that to happen.

"Nope. We're divorced," she told him.

"Terminal boredom, huh? I told you."

"Not exactly," she said, thinking of Mack's fling that had made her life anything but boring. "Another long story."

"So what's up?"

"I need a favor."

"Anything. I owe you big-time for helping me nail that bastard in New York a few years back. The guy's still rotting in jail, contemplating his sins against all those folks he lured into buying junk bonds with their life savings."

"Have you checked on that lately? He's probably out and back in business. I hear the industry's not that attentive to policing its own. I saw a story not long ago in the *L.A. Times* indicating that some of the worst checked out just fine on an industry hotline meant to identify the bad guys."

"Things always were lax, or none of those guys would have gotten away with as much as they did. Anyway, what's up? You want out of Georgia?"

"Only temporarily. I need to get to Armand LeConte. If you can tell me how to storm the fortress I hear he has out there, I'll be on the next flight to Dulles."

Chad whistled. "You don't want much, do you? What's Armand into down your way? Selling Uzis and AK forty-sevens to the peanut farmers?"

"Maybe nothing. I just figured he'd be a starting point."

"Ah, Amanda, you always did like to start at the top," he said with a trace of admiration. "Most journalists follow trails that eventually wind up at LeConte. You want to start there. You going to tell me what this is about?"

"If it turns out to be anything at all, I'll pass it on to you first."

"But not now?"

"Sorry. Not now."

"How about this? You fly in. I'll make the arrangements with LeConte and drive you out there."

Amanda grinned at the obvious ploy. "Chad, Chad, you used to be so subtle."

"When it comes to LeConte, I don't waste time on finesse. If you have something, I want in."

"In due time. I'll play fair with you, I promise."

"I could always tail you from the airport and hide in the bushes."

She wasn't at all sure he was joking. "First you have to figure out when I'm coming in. Are you going to help me out here or not? I can always ask the network to run some of your old footage, get a good glimpse of his estate, rent a helicopter, and fly around until I spot it."

"You would, too, wouldn't you?" he said with a laugh. "Okay. Save yourself the headache, sweetheart. I'll give you a number. I can't guarantee he'll see you, though on second thought you're female and beautiful. That should get you in the door. Of course, it might also keep you from getting out again." He gave her the carefully guarded phone number and address, then his tone sobered. "Be careful, Amanda. The man does have a certain reputation with women."

"If you knew the mood I'm in about your gender, you wouldn't worry."

"I'll bet there's yet another fascinating story behind that."

"Not so fascinating. Thanks for the number, Chad. I'll be in touch."

"Call when you're in town. I'll take you to the fanciest restaurant in D.C. and ply you with champagne and fine food."

"All the while trying to trick me into telling me what's going on with LeConte. No thanks. We'll do it another time." She hung up before he came up with any other bright ideas about ways to get in on her exclusive.

She studied the address and phone number for several minutes, debating whether to call for an interview or surprise LeConte with a personal visit. On one hand, she had a feeling he might not be the kind of man who liked surprises. On the other hand, catching him with his guard down might cause him to reveal more.

Still holding the piece of paper, she went into Oscar's office. He glanced up from his computer screen. "You ever heard of knocking?"

"Are you writing dirty lyrics on your terminal?"

He glared at her. She grinned back. "Then what's the big deal?"

"Etiquette, Amanda. Office Etiquette."

"This is a magazine, Oscar. Not a charm school."

Still looking sour, he ignored the sarcasm. "Now that you're in here, interrupting me in the middle of editing our lead story for next month—a story that you did write, I might add—you might as well say what's on your mind."

"Armand LeConte."

His eyes widened behind his reading glasses. "You found him already?"

"I found him. Now I want to fly to Washington to

talk to him." Although *Inside Atlanta*'s publisher had reasonably lenient ideas about expense accounts, Oscar did not. He was as tight-fisted as a pensioner on a budget. She waited for the inevitable lecture on phoning versus traveling.

Instead, he looked for her straight in the eye, nodded, and said, "Okay."

"Okay?" she repeated, unable to mask her disbelief. "You wanted me to turn you down?"

"No, of course not, but—"

"Amanda, if this story pans out, you can put this magazine on the map. I'd say that's worth airfare to D.C."

"Thank you," she said, backing out the door before he could change his mind.

"Fly coach," he hollered after her.

That was more like it, she thought as she went back to her desk and began making plans. The only thing she'd forgotten was her mother. Obviously a Freudian slip, she thought later as she listened to her horrified parent think of a dozen reasons why she shouldn't traipse off to see LeConte alone.

"Amanda, I didn't mean for you to go out to that man's house," her mother said. "He's an international arms dealer, for God's sake."

"I'm going to interview him, not buy guns."

"Didn't you see Chad's story about that house? It's in the middle of a hundred acres with guard dogs all around and every security system known to man. You can't just walk up and knock on the door."

"I'll call and make an appointment."

"Oh. I suppose that makes sense." Her face fell. "And what should I do while you're gone?"

Suddenly Amanda realized exactly why her mother had reversed that morning's breakthrough. She felt as if she were being abandoned all over again, this time by the daughter with whom she'd sought refuge.

"Mother, you have a job now. You'll stay right here. I'll be back before you even notice I'm gone. You'll have some time alone to think." The reassurance didn't have the desired effect. Her mother scowled at her.

"If I had wanted to be alone, I could have stayed in that outrageously overpriced hotel in Manhattan. At least then I had the satisfaction of knowing that your father would have to pay the bills."

Making allowances for her mother's fragile state, Amanda refused to get drawn into a quarrel. "I'm sorry. I know this is a rough time for you, but I have to make this trip. With any luck I won't be gone more than a day or two."

Her mother sighed heavily, every bit of progress they'd made earlier forgotten as she sank into martyrdom. "I suppose I could manage that long, even though I don't know a soul."

Despite herself, Amanda felt a tiny twinge of guilt. She stomped on it. She needed to go to Washington for her own peace of mind almost as badly as she needed to go there to interview Armand LeConte. She needed a change of scenery. She needed the change of perspective. And she definitely needed the challenge of this story. Her mother's needs would have to wait. She'd be in better shape to deal with them when she returned.

"Come on, Mother. Drive me to the airport."

"Why don't you take the car? You can leave it there."

"And then how will you get to work tomorrow?"

"I didn't think you'd want me to go in."

"Mother, I got you a job. I didn't put you in daycare. Don't you dare let me down."

Her mother's expression brightened even more quickly

than it had dimmed, proving that she'd feared feeling useless more than she'd feared being left alone. She grabbed the car keys with renewed enthusiasm. "Let's go then. You don't know how lucky you are to have these lovely roads."

"The roads are no different than New York's. Down here we just don't put as many people on them."

"I know. I can't remember the last time I was able to drive seventy on an expressway."

Grinning, Amanda decided not to remind her mother that the speed limit was considerably less than that. Or at least that's what the police kept telling her. This visit was turning into a real eye-opener as she realized just how many personality traits she and her mother shared.

It was too late to call LeConte by the time Amanda's much-delayed flight reached Dulles Airport. She got a room at a nearby hotel and spent the evening mapping out her strategy for approaching him. First thing in the morning, hoping he wasn't any more alert then than she usually was, she dialed the number that Chad had given her. She wasn't sure exactly what she'd expected, a French maid perhaps, but it definitely wasn't the cheerful hello of a child. She sounded about six.

"Is this the LeConte residence?" Amanda asked cautiously.

"Yes," the girl said, suddenly sounding shy. "Do you want to talk to my daddy?"

"Yes, please." Amanda couldn't believe her good fortune. A secretary or bodyguard would have had her jumping through hoops.

"I'll get him," the little girl said. Then her running footsteps clattered happily over wooden floors.

It occurred to Amanda as she waited that the child's

father might be someone other than LeConte himself, but the voice that came on the line moments later oozed that French *je ne sais quoi* that set the arms dealer apart from other men. If she hadn't been on assignment and well aware of the man's chosen career, she might have melted on the spot. She was silent for so long as she indulged in wishful thinking that he nearly hung up.

"Is anyone there?" he demanded with evident impatience.

If Amanda had been wearing tap shoes, she would have clicked the heels together in dutiful obedience. Instead, she introduced herself and requested an interview.

"Where exactly are you from?" he asked as if he were unfamiliar with Georgia.

Amanda repeated the information. "I'm at a hotel near Dulles now. I could be at your place in an hour, maybe less, depending on how long it takes me to rent a car."

"I'm sorry you have come all this way for nothing, but I do not do interviews."

"This wouldn't be an interview," she said hurriedly. "Exactly."

"What *exactly* would it be?"

"A conversation. Chad Keyes said you might be willing to consider that."

"Ah, so you know Monsieur Keyes?"

Amanda hadn't been sure what reaction the mention of Chad's name would draw. It seemed, though, that LeConte's voice held a note that hovered somewhere between respect and even greater caution. She guessed it was the wariness of a man who knew his enemies well and admired their skill and cunning.

"He is an old friend," Amanda assured him. "We have worked together on stories in the past."

"I will check this, of course."

Amanda smiled at the warning. He'd probably have an entire dossier on her before she could reach the grounds. "Of course," she agreed.

He paused, then inquired carefully, "This conversation, then, it would be off the record?"

"For background only, if that's the way you want it," she agreed, figuring she needed knowledge that he had far more than she needed a rare interview for publication. Besides, if he said something she needed for attribution, she trusted in her powers of persuasion to talk him into letting her use it.

"Why should I trust you?"

Given Amanda's personal experience with broken trust, she didn't have a solid answer for him on that. "In your business, I'm sure you have to be a good judge of people to survive," she improvised. "Meet me and then make your judgment."

He chuckled. "Ah, *madame*, I see you possess both confidence and daring. I find that very attractive in a woman. Come along, then. I will tell my associates to let you through."

As she hung up, Amanda tried to temper her sense of triumph. Any man who'd paired *attractive* and *woman* in the same sentence when agreeing to anything was a man to be watched. She recalled the warnings both Chad and her mother had given her about LeConte's amorous tendencies.

By the same token, a child underfoot implied a wife nearby, she reassured herself. And then she drove straight into the wolf's den.

# CHAPTER

## Ten

AFTER the peaceful country scenery of rolling hills and leaves turning the vibrant autumn hues of red, orange, and gold under an Indian summer sky of purest blue, the stark black iron gate guarding Armand LeConte's estate had a chilling effect. The man with the gun didn't help. He looked as if he were itching to use it. Amanda was no expert on weapons, but this one looked powerful enough to blow her into the next county in little bitty pieces.

With a hawklike nose and eyes as black as onyx, the guard cast a fierce, forbidding gaze at Amanda, asked to see her driver's license to prove her identification, then directed her inside.

"Follow the drive to the right. It will take you to the main house," he said. "Mr. LeConte is expecting you."

His cold expression told her exactly what he thought of Mr. LeConte's decision to see her. She smiled anyway.

"Thanks," she said, not because he'd done anything deserving of her appreciation, but simply because he hadn't used that ominous gun.

The man who answered the door of the rambling white farmhouse was only slightly more reassuring. His expression mirrored the guard's, but he didn't have a gun. At least not where Amanda could detect it. If it wasn't on his person, though, she had a hunch he knew where to find one in a hurry. Either everyone out here was paranoid or it was considered pro forma to flash around the same guns the boss dealt in. Sort of in-house advertising.

She was directed into an office with a sweeping view of the rolling hills that took her breath away. She was contemplating the wonder of being able to swivel around and watch the seasons change outside the succession of French doors that made up the entire back wall, when she heard a whisper of sound. Glancing around nervously, she saw a pair of wide blue eyes peering back at her from under the desk.

"Hi."

There was a hint of impishness in the shy little voice that floated up to her. Amanda couldn't contain a grin. She hunkered down until she was on eye level. "Hi, yourself. Are you in charge around here?"

The question was greeted with a giggle. "No. I'm too little."

"Size and age have nothing to do with power, *ma petite*," a laughter-filled male voice lectured gently.

Here, clearly, was a man after her own heart, Amanda thought. She stood up slowly and caught the spark of tolerant amusement in Armand LeConte's crystal-blue eyes. In that instant she recognized the full power of his charisma. It had little to do with looks, although he was attractive in a lean and hungry way. It was his presence, that lazy self-confidence and the intelligence burning in his eyes. Her pulse leaped, even as her brain went on full, self-protective alert. Here was a dangerous, seductive man who knew exactly how to get whatever—or whomever—he wanted in life.

With his intense gaze clashing with hers, he took her proffered hand and raised it slowly to his lips. The caress was quick, not lingering, but Amanda felt as if she'd been branded by the hint of intimacy. It was an unnerving sensation, especially for a woman who'd claimed only a few short hours ago to be immune to men.

"Mr. LeConte, thank you for seeing me," she said, practically tumbling into the nearest chair, a Queen Anne side chair that encouraged decorum. More important, it was separated from the wing chair behind his desk by an impressive stretch of glass-topped mahogany. She wanted that distance. In fact, she had a feeling that in another five minutes she'd be demanding a chaperon. Even the subtly provocative fabric of the man's shirt somehow reminded her of the texture of the finest sheets and had her conjuring up wicked images of tumbling around on those very sheets.

With him.

Heaven help her!

To her regret, he took the chair next to her, stretching his long legs out in front of him in a relaxed posture that deliberately counterpointed her obvious tension. She hurriedly reached for her tape recorder to remind herself of exactly what she was doing here.

"Off the record," he chided, even as he rested his hand atop the head of the child who'd come to stand at his side, her elbows resting on his knee, the folds of her crisply pressed dress falling nearly to the floor. She was the picture of pint-sized femininity in a way that American children rarely were, except under duress. Amanda couldn't help wondering if she was ever allowed outside to play on the grass or whether she'd ever come home streaked with ice cream and mustard and cotton candy.

LeConte glanced down at his daughter with an expression of bemusement. He brushed a stray wisp of soft brown hair from that delicate face with its astonishing mature expression of self-containment then said, "Run along, *ma petite*. I have business now."

To Amanda's delight, the child actually gave a quick little bobbing curtsy as she said, "Yes, Papa," Then she gave Amanda a grin and scampered away, the tap of her patent leather shoes finally fading into the distance.

"She is a beautiful child," Amanda said.

"Yes. Noelle is the one true joy in my life," he said with an odd trace of melancholy in his tone and a faraway look in his eyes. Jane Austen or the Brontë sisters could have written volumes about that brooding look.

Amanda didn't doubt for an instant that the hint of some deep, personal tragedy was genuine. She also recognized it as a powerful lure for most women. No female could be around such subtle sorrow in an otherwise strong, resilient man without wanting to make things right, without wanting to mother that child and soothe the father. If she didn't get the information she'd come after and hightail it out of there, she might volunteer herself. No wonder Chad's warning had seemed so urgent.

"What can I do for you, Amanda? I may call you Amanda?" LeConte flashed her a smile that surely had melted colder resolve than hers.

"Please," she found herself saying, though professionalism and common sense told her she ought to be keeping this interview so formal it could pass muster under Emily Post's scrutiny, to say nothing of Oscar's.

His gaze caught hers again and deliberately held it, as if he enjoyed the knowledge that he was unnerving her. "You were going to tell me why you wished to see me," he prodded, a hint of teasing laughter back in his tone.

"Yes, of course," she said, feeling more fumbling and awkward than she had on her first date. When she realized that he'd probably set out to encourage that exact response, she gathered her composure and said briskly, "Actually, it's about guns."

His expression suggested that the statement wasn't to be taken seriously. "*Ma chérie*, if you wish a pistol with which to protect yourself, I am sure there are many places in Georgia which could provide one."

"I have a gun," she said, then regretted the admission when she saw his nod of approval. He'd have her practicing on a gun range if she wasn't careful. He probably had one set up on the property for all those armed minions he kept around.

"I usually can't find it," she added in a rush. "Obviously I have no need of more."

"If not for yourself, what then? You do not look as if you wish to purchase a supply for an army. Or do you harbor tendencies toward insurrection I cannot imagine?"

Amanda ignored the teasing, patronizing tone for once in her life. "No, but I was hoping you could tell me how one would go about that."

"What makes you think I would know such a thing?" he parried.

Amanda couldn't help grinning at his deliberately innocent expression. Only someone terribly naïve would buy it. Clearly he didn't expect her to, but he seemed to enjoy the challenge of baiting her.

"Let's say for the moment you are my star witness," she countered. "I, like the court, would be willing to testify to your expertise in this area. I'm not here to report on that. I'm here because I need help in tracing a deal that is purportedly going on in Atlanta."

"I have no business in Atlanta," he said flatly.

"But the word is that you are well connected. I'm sure you know who might."

She hadn't said it to flatter him, but he seemed pleased by the acknowledgment just the same.

"Perhaps you should fill me in on exactly what you think you know. Then, because I like you, if it is possible I will corroborate or deny."

Amanda nodded. "Fair enough."

She told him everything that had happened, from the anonymous phone call to the meeting in the cemetery, the shooting, the disappearance of the body, and the fact that she was 99 percent certain that the dead man was Richard Howell, who had worked for the National Bank of the Netherlands.

The last trace of benevolent amusement faded during her recitation. A hard glint came into his eyes. "And you believe that all of this indicates that someone is selling military technology of some sort to the Iraqis, despite this country's very specific laws precluding such acts?"

"Do you have a better explanation?"

"Perhaps it is merely the product of an overactive

imagination, the theory of a young banker who had grown bored with his life. Perhaps he merely twisted this so-called evidence to suit his fancies.''

"I suppose that is possible, but I don't think so.''

"Why is that?''

"Because he is dead, the bank gets very nervous when I ask about him, and the FBI is having apoplexy over the fact that I know anything at all. Now, personally, I don't have a problem with giving the FBI fits, but I'd prefer to know exactly what I'm dealing with here.''

"Yes, I can see that," he said, regarding her with some regret. "I am sorry, however, that I cannot be of help.''

"Cannot or won't?''

He shrugged. "Perhaps some of each. Perhaps my understanding of what happens in Georgia is limited. It is, after all, beyond the scope of my normal activities. Perhaps I would not like to see such a lovely young woman become involved in something potentially dangerous.''

"Mr. LeConte, it's dangerous just to get in a car and get on the freeway these days. Trust me when I say I can take care of myself.''

He chuckled. "Ah, *ma chérie*, I am sure you believe that. I am equally certain that you do not understand the ways of the people involved in a scenario such as the one you are describing. They would kill you without thinking twice, just as they did that young man.''

"That may be so," Amanda argued, "though I suspect I know more about what motivates people to kill than you credit me with knowing. It would not be the first time I have challenged someone desperate enough to wish me harm. It is up to me whether to take the risk.''

He offered a rueful smile. "No. In this instance, I believe it is up to me."

Amanda had met enough stubborn, protective men in her time to know that she had gotten all she was going to get from LeConte, at least for the moment. Either he knew no more or he had determined not to share it with her for her own protection. In retrospect it was ironic that she'd worried about the difficulty of getting in to see Armand LeConte. That, as it had turned out, had been the easy part. Getting information from him had been something else altogether. In fact, if anything he probably had gained more from the interview than she had.

She was absolutely certain that if he had been unfamiliar with the deal they'd been discussing before her arrival, he would know every last detail by the end of the day. Perhaps then she could try again to persuade him to share that information with her. Until then it would be a waste of her energy.

She stood up, grateful to be ending the disconcerting interview. "Thank you for your time."

He looked surprised by her easy acquiescence. "No arguments?"

Amanda shrugged. "Would there be any point?"

"No, but I do enjoy battling wits with a beautiful woman."

"Some other time."

He stood and took her hand again. "I will hold you to that, *ma chérie*."

Although she hadn't seen him press any sort of buzzer, the man who'd admitted her to the house materialized along with another man who looked as if he'd been turned out from the same watchdog mold.

"*Au revoir*," LeConte said. "It has been my pleas-

ure.'' The warmth of his intense gaze confirmed his
sincerity.

What worried Amanda more than the predatory gleam
in his eyes, however, was the knowledge that despite
her failure to gain one piece of useful information, she
had enjoyed the meeting every bit as much as he had.

# CHAPTER

## *Eleven*

IT had all been too simple. Even taking into account his cautious reticence, LeConte had been too trusting. Amanda knew that even if he had been fascinated with her as a woman, he would never simply let things rest. She wondered, in fact, if he might decide that she knew just enough to be troublesome. There was one way to find out.

Under the watchful eyes of the armed guard, she dutifully drove through the gate of LeConte's estate. But instead of racing on, she went a few hundred yards out of sight, then turned into an unmarked lane to see if anyone came after her, as she suspected they might.

Sure enough, moments later a sleek sports car tore through the gate and skidded onto the highway on two wheels. Obviously the driver hadn't anticipated the speediness of her departure. Jeffrey Dunne or Jim Harrison could have warned him, if he'd been on speaking terms with the FBI or the Atlanta PD. Judging from his expression, which she was able to glimpse as he sped past, he was worried about the cost of his misjudgment. For all of Armand LeConte's tenderness with his child, the arms dealer hadn't struck her as the sort of man who tolerated screw-ups.

When the pursuing car was out of sight, Amanda drove back onto the highway at a more deliberate pace. It wasn't until she was within a few miles of Dulles Airport that she realized her evasive tactics hadn't been quite as successful as she'd thought. She might have lost the sports car, but a bland gray sedan had taken up following a discreet two cars back. Something about that car triggered an alarm.

Although she told herself she was being every bit as paranoid as the man whose home she'd just left, she zipped into the passing lane, accelerated, and tried to put a few more cars between her and that worrisome sedan. Watching in the side mirror, she saw the car swerve into the outside lane, catch up to within two cars, then pull back in behind her, proving her suspicions. Although she couldn't get a clear view of much beyond the headlights, the vague shape, and the color, she recognized the type of car. Jeffrey Dunne had one just like it. She had a hunch it was pretty much standard issue FBI.

Wasn't it fascinating, she thought, that the FBI had apparently followed her to LeConte's? Although it probably wasn't the agency's intention, it lent a certain credence to her investigation. As exasperating as it was being tailed, she found that she was more pleased than annoyed.

No sooner had she spotted what she was sure was an

FBI tail, than LeConte's minion materialized from a side road. He joined in the parade. Amanda began to feel like the Pied Piper.

She had just made her turn into the brightly lit rental-car lot ten minutes later when a black sedan swerved in front of the other two cars trailing her, the driver's gaze pinned on her. Horns blared and tires squealed. Amanda shook her head at the macho nonsense. She parked, got out of the car and waved blithely, then started across the lot.

She had gone a hundred feet, was almost through the door in fact, when a shot rang out and the plate glass window in front of her shattered, sending a spray of glass all over her. She felt something nick her face, just as arms enveloped her in a full-body tackle that sent her sprawling on the ground amid all those shards of glass, some total stranger draped protectively over her. Thank God for long pants and long sleeves, she thought as she hit the ground.

"What the hell?" she muttered indignantly, trying to shove the person off, while avoiding further serious damage from all that glass.

"Stay still, dammit."

Lately only one man's voice carried that exact note of exasperation when addressing her: Jeffrey Dunne. How the hell had he tracked her to Virginia, when she'd left town with virtually no notice?

"What are you doing here?" Amanda asked, making it a point to remain very still beneath him. He didn't seem in the mood to put up with a break for freedom. Besides, she had no desire to add to her injuries. She could already feel a trickle of blood on her cheek.

"Oh, I thought I'd fly up to Washington, take a little drive in the country, see how long it would be before I could engage in a little gunplay. It's the way I always spend my days off," he said, waving off several people who'd gathered to offer help.

"I didn't think people like you took days off," Amanda retorted.

"It was the only way I could follow you up here in an unofficial capacity."

"Why would you want to do that? Usually you can't wait to see the last of me."

"Not so, Amanda. As for my reasons, let's just say I get a very weird feeling in my gut when the name Armand LeConte creeps into any conversation in polite company."

Amanda did wriggle out from under him then, moving cautiously through the glass. "What conversation was that?" she demanded suspiciously while searching her purse for one of Grandmother Hunt's lace-edged hankies to blot the cut on her face. It would probably be ruined, she thought regretfully as she dabbed at the blood.

Dunne winced at the question. "Never mind."

Her eyes widened as she considered the possibilities. Only one made sense. "You have my phone tapped, don't you?" She hauled her arm back to slug him, but he was more nimble than she'd guessed. He dodged her fist, grabbed a wrist, and hauled her back to the ground. "Stay low, you little idiot."

"What makes you think that shot was aimed at me?"

"You see anyone else around on the ground? That bullet whizzed so close to your head, if you'd sneezed you would have bumped right into it."

"Okay, let's assume it was meant for me, though personally I can imagine a lot more people finding you irritating. Exactly who was shooting this gun?"

"That's the tough part. I didn't get a good look at them. I don't suppose you have any ideas?"

"I didn't see where it came from. You know, there is another possibility. It could be that they were shooting at each other."

"They?"

She ignored his obvious fascination. "Did the shot come from a red sports car?"

"No. A gray sedan."

She blinked. "I thought you were in the gray sedan."

"Not me. I just got here. Haven't even filled out a car rental form yet."

"Then who the hell was in the gray sedan?"

"Amanda, that was my question, remember?"

"What about the black car?"

"Didn't see it. What the hell were you doing? Leading a parade?"

"Seemed that way to me," she confessed. "If I'd known how irritable the participants were going to get, I'd have asked for a police escort."

"Next time maybe you ought to do just that," he said, finally holding out his hand and helping her to her feet.

Amanda glanced around the rental agency parking lot. Her bevy of admirers seemed to have vanished.

"Looks like it's just you and me," she observed as she dropped her express rental contract into the box. "I think I'll let you explain about all this glass."

"Where do you think you're going?" he demanded, marching across the parking lot after her.

"I'm going to be on the next flight back to Atlanta. How about you? Planning to go back or drop in on your bosses across the river? Might's well use the trip to make brownie points, so it won't be a total loss."

He glared at her. "Come on," he said, leading her into the airport. He waited while she made a quick call to her mother to let her know she'd finished up in Virginia and would be back later that night.

As they walked to the gate, he said with feigned cheer, "Won't this be fun? We can be seatmates and you can fill me in on your meeting with LeConte."

Amanda shook her head. "I don't think so. Why not wait until I tell someone about it over the phone?"

"Amanda, I didn't set up the wiretap."

"Then who did?"

"The orders came from above me."

"Office or home?"

"Both."

"Jesus. And here I thought this was the land of the free."

"It is, as long as you don't go against your government."

Amanda scowled at him. "Look, I'm not the one selling arms or military technology to the enemy. I'm trying to find out who did and who let them get away with it. I don't suppose you'd know anything about that, would you?"

To his credit, Jeffrey Dunne didn't outright lie to her. He just settled into a silent funk. The irony was that he was probably every bit as much in the dark about all this as she was and probably just as outraged. They'd had a long talk one night during that last case. She knew how strongly he felt about catching the bad guys. It would offend him deeply to discover that someone above him was actually assisting them.

"You know," she said eventually, when they both had a drink in hand. "You could help me with this."

He glanced over at her. "I don't think so."

"You came to Washington on your own. Why?"

"I told you. Because of LeConte."

"Are you sure it's not because you know as well as I do that someone's playing fast and loose with military technology and the government's either involved directly or giving tacit approval to it?"

"You don't know that."

"Not yet, but I will prove it sooner or later. Sooner, if I have your help."

He shook his head. "Sorry. No can do."

Amanda shrugged at the expected display of stubbornness. "Too bad. I thought you'd want to nail the suckers."

"I do," he said. "But I have to do it my own way."

"And that means behind closed doors, not in the pages of a magazine. Is that it?"

"Something like that."

"Hasn't it ever occurred to you that not much ever changes until the public gets wind of it? Then the people on Capitol Hill get scared and clean up their act. As long as they can sweep it under the carpet, it doesn't exist. The Clarence Thomas–Anita Hill debacle is a perfect example. The Senate was willing to look the other way, until someone leaked it to the media and said, 'Hey, we have a problem here.'"

She gave him a rueful look. "Of course, the whole nature of your business operates on a need-to-know basis. It's probably no wonder you don't think the public has a right to know what sort of shenanigans its officials are into."

"Is this the start of a lecture on public policy and the media? If so, I'm not up for it."

"Because you know your position is indefensible."

"No, Amanda," he said flatly. "I don't know that at all."

Just before he closed his eyes, however, Amanda was almost positive she caught a glimpse of uncertainty. Perhaps she had shaken the complacency of one FBI agent after all. She considered it her good deed for the day.

It was well after midnight when Amanda finally got home. With planes stacked up in Atlanta waiting out a storm drifting over the entire Southeast, the delay in the air had seemed endless. Finding her mother huddled under a blanket on her living room sofa, her face still damp with tears, made Amanda's heart wrench. She debated whether to wake her and send her to bed or leave her where she was now that she'd finally fallen asleep. Unfortunately, the decision was taken out of her hands as her mother stirred.

"Amanda, you're home. I tried to wait up. What time is it?"

"Nearly twelve-thirty. Mother, you look absolutely exhausted. Why don't you go on in to bed? I'll bring you a cup of herbal tea."

Her mother shook her head. "If I drink one more cup of tea, I'll float away. Your friend Miss Martha dropped by earlier. She made at least three pots of the stuff."

Miss Martha Wellington was an octogenarian busybody who'd made Amanda's state of mind her personal mission ever since the canceled wedding with Donelli. Amanda wasn't surprised to hear she'd dropped by. She'd probably nearly swooned with delight to find yet another person to comfort. It almost made Amanda grateful for her mother's presence. Maybe it would take the heat off of her.

"Did the two of you talk?"

"She talked. I listened. Dear, you are so lucky to have such lovely friends who care so much. I'm afraid I let your father become my whole world. And now..." Her hands fluttered helplessly.

Amanda really wasn't up for any more soul-searching talks. "Mother, it's late. We don't have to talk about this now," she said, unable to hide the note of desperation in her voice. She did not want to hear more details tonight. She wasn't sure she wanted to hear them ever. For a reporter normally addicted to facts, she was suddenly surprisingly tolerant of the concept of evasiveness.

Her mother's sad eyes met hers. Ignoring Amanda's plea or simply unable to keep silent any longer, she said, "Do you know I sat in that hospital day after day when your father was in intensive care wondering what on earth I would do if I ever lost him? I realized how much I needed him, how much I still loved him."

A flash of anger was there and gone so quickly that Amanda wondered if she'd imagined it, until she heard the change in her mother's tone.

"Do you know what he was thinking?" she demanded indignantly. "Do you? Well, all that time the man I've loved more than life itself was trying to come up with ways to get rid of me."

Shocked by the implication, Amanda simply stared. She finally rallied sufficiently to protest, "Mother, I'm sure you're wrong."

"I'm telling you, your father started thinking about divorce while he was still on his deathbed. He had one of those midlife revelations or something. At least that's what he says. I say he's probably got some little tramp he's hot for."

Amanda thought of the music she'd heard when she called the house and had a sudden vision of her father and *some little tramp* engaging in hot pursuits. She shuddered.

"Not Dad," she said with considerably less certainty than she would have liked. He hadn't denied her charge about the bimbo. He'd hung up on her.

"He's a man, isn't he?" her mother said bitterly.

"Mother, do you really have any reason to believe there's another woman?"

"You mean have I caught him in the act? No, of course not. Your father is much too discreet for that. That doesn't mean she doesn't exist. Why else would he want a divorce out of the blue like this?"

Amanda had absolutely no answer for that. "He was sick, Mother. Maybe he just got scared and started reevaluating his life and didn't like what he saw."

"You mean his marriage to me."

"I mean everything. Maybe he just felt like starting over. I can relate to the feeling. That's how I felt after Mack left. I questioned everything. It's happening to me again now. That's what traumatic events do to you. They make you take stock."

"Oh, for heaven's sake, don't you think I know that?" her mother retorted impatiently. "Amanda, my life hasn't always been so perfect. There was a time when I wondered if I was throwing away my chance for real happiness and fulfillment because I didn't have a career. That didn't make me walk out the door on a commitment."

Amanda was stunned to discover that her mother had ever seriously contemplated a career. She had always seemed so content with her charities and her social engagements, with the life she and Amanda's father had built together. "Mother, if you felt like that, why didn't you just go out and get a job?"

"Your father wouldn't hear of it. He was providing for us more than adequately. He couldn't imagine why I wanted to work."

"Then maybe you should have left."

"Maybe so," she said with a sigh. "But I guess in the end I didn't feel that strongly about it. I weighed what I had with your father and made the choice to stay."

"No regrets?"

"Not really. Not until now, when I see that I stayed for nothing."

"But don't you see, Mother? You've been through your self-evaluation. You've made your decision. Up until now, Dad hasn't questioned anything. It sounds like that's what he's doing now. Don't you think you should be a little more compassionate about this turmoil he's in?"

"He's not in turmoil, Amanda. He's embracing this separation. He's having the time of his life."

So that was the bottom line. Her mother had chosen to stay. Her father had not. And no doubt she resented his decision all the more because it wasn't the same one she had made.

"I'm sorry, Mother."

This time her mother's sigh was filled with weary resignation. "So am I, darling. So am I."

# CHAPTER

## *Twelve*

**T**HERE were days, even months, when Amanda wished that investigative reporting were as easy or as glamorous as it was made out to be on TV and in the movies. Instead, all too much time was spent on tedious searches for one tiny shred of information that might lead to the eventual unraveling of an entire scam. That slow, meticulous gathering of facts was something journalists shared with private investigators and detectives. Only rarely did they get lucky.

Now, since Armand LeConte had remained slyly coy about any knowledge he might have of Iraqi arms deals played out in Atlanta, Amanda was stuck with doing things the hard way.

Selecting a handful of her favorite jelly beans from the jar on her desk, she shoved aside stacks of accumulated files. She ignored the ones that fell on the floor.

She spread out a dozen newspaper clippings on the prior, much publicized case and studied them again. If this particular story followed the pattern of the previously alleged link between Iraq and that Italian bank, then there should be companies around Atlanta that had been doing deals that wouldn't stand up under the glare of too much scrutiny.

Which companies, though? Selling what? Financed by whom? And how had they gotten government approval to ship the questionable technology?

*Inside Atlanta* had recently hired a top-notch business reporter. Jack Davis had been covering the financial scene in town for the local papers and for business publications for the last twenty years. Oscar Cates and Joel Crenshaw had been trying to recruit him for more than a year but hadn't been able to match the accumulated perks of his tenure. He'd finally accepted a month ago. There had been a great deal of speculation among the envious staff about exactly what combination of money, benefits, and promises of editorial freedom it had taken to snag him.

She glanced across the newsroom and studied him. Based on his credentials alone, Jack had to be in his early forties, but he looked ten years younger. Blue eyes peered owlishly through bottle-thick glasses. He was thin and rumpled and had the nervous energy of someone who drank half a dozen cups of coffee before noon.

Despite all that wired tension, Jack Davis had a voice and manner that could cajole secrets from a priest. As she neared his desk, Amanda listened admiringly as he patiently worked a source, nudging gently, prodding carefully. All the while his pencil tapped a staccato rhythm that belied his cautious inquiry.

There was probably a lesson to be learned here, she

noted ruefully. She would have been shouting and demanding long before now. And, unlike Jack, who was suddenly scrawling notes at a rapidfire clip, she would have come away with only her irritation to show for the interview.

He was smiling with satisfaction when he finally hung up several minutes later.

"Nice job," she said.

He jerked his head up and nearly lost his glasses. Flustered, he nabbed them and shoved them back in place. "Amanda, I didn't know you were standing there. Have you been waiting long?"

"Long enough to watch you in action. I'm impressed."

"Just doing my job," he said modestly, an embarrassed flush creeping into his cheeks. "Sometimes I have to remind them that it's more important to give the story to someone who'll report it accurately than it is to give it to the reporter with the biggest circulation. It's tough for a monthly to beat the weekly and daily competition, but it can be done."

She drew up a chair. "Do you have a minute?"

"Sure. I guess. What can I do for you?"

"I need to tap your brain. I'm working on a story with a business angle. I need to know what companies in the Atlanta area might manufacture equipment that could serve a dual purpose."

Jack's awkwardness vanished immediately as he moved into his arena of expertise. "Dual like what? Computers that could serve a business function or become a component of military equipment? That sort of thing?"

"Exactly."

"There are several, depending on whether you're looking for software, computer technology, machinery."

"I'm not sure of the specifics. Has anyone gotten a

major overseas contract, added a lot of staff, tried to keep their production under wraps when you've been doing routine queries? Anything suspicious?''

He blinked rapidly as the implications of her questions sank in. ''What on earth are you working on?''

''I can't say just yet, but you could save me a lot of time if you could think of some businesses that have grown suspiciously lately or acted awfully tight-lipped about something that should have been perfectly aboveboard.''

''Let me think a minute.'' He leaned back in his swivel chair and stared at the ceiling for so long that Amanda wondered if he'd nodded off. Suddenly his chair tipped back into place and he reached for the middle drawer of the file cabinet beside his desk.

''I got a release,'' he muttered. ''Six months ago I think it was.''

He flipped through the neatly labeled, orderly files, unerringly seizing one that was just where he expected it to be. Given the state of her own desk, Amanda was awed.

''Here it is,'' he said, handing her the single page with a flashy logo.

''What's so odd about this particular release?'' Amanda asked as she glanced over the enthusiastically worded announcement of an expansion at Sunland Electronics. It looked like any one of a hundred releases that passed through an office like this in a month. The ones that crossed her desk generally landed in the circular file. She was deeply grateful that Jack was less cavalier with the material that crossed his.

''On the surface, nothing. But I was interested. I called to check it out. Thought about going out to do a feature since it's a small company that looked like it was poised to make a breakthrough into the big leagues.''

''And?''

"And when I called, I got a runaround. I was told the announcement was premature. The PR guy who'd written the release was suddenly unavailable for comment. All calls were referred to the company president and he stonewalled me, even though our relationship in the past had been pretty solid. The whole thing struck me as ridiculous given the fact that it was some business-page feature I was after and not some big exposé."

"Why did you drop it if you thought it was so odd?"

"Amanda, I have a file of stories an inch thick that I haven't had time to get to. I can't possibly chase after all of them. Besides, I just figured the PR person had gotten it wrong. Happens all the time. I would never have thought of it again, if you hadn't prodded my memory just now."

"Who'd you talk to out there?"

"Calvin Jones is the president. He founded the company ten years ago. An interesting guy. Impoverished background. Overcame all sorts of odds just to get to college at Georgia Tech. Worked internships at a few companies around town. One of the places took a special interest in his career, hired him on after graduation, boosted him up the corporate ladder. Ten years later he borrowed against everything he owned to start up Sunland. Got a couple of modest government contracts along the way, but with the federal budget tightening and the economy struggling, he's taken a hit the past couple of years. I was pleased for him when I saw the release."

"Can I hang on to this?" Amanda asked.

Jack reached for it. "I'll make you a copy."

He dashed across the newsroom to the copier. He handed her a copy on his return, then tucked the original safely back in its file.

Sunland Electronics. Amanda signed on to the computer and checked for other stories in the data base. She found the one on Calvin Jones's career. It had been in the business section of the *Constitution* a few years back. Jack Davis had written it. It was a fascinating profile of a smart, aggressive young black man who'd beaten the odds.

Beyond that, there was only a small news story about financial problems at Sunland—staff cutbacks and the threat of bankruptcy. A last-minute infusion of cash only weeks before that troublesome press release had staved off the need to file for Chapter 11. Jack had written that as well, but it had been buried, as if he'd wanted to do all he could to protect a man he'd admired from humiliation.

She made copies of both articles, then called the National Bank of the Netherlands and asked for Jenny Lee. Oscar had told her first thing this morning that the receptionist had been hired late the preceding afternoon and had agreed to start immediately.

"Congratulations," Amanda said, when she had her on the line.

"I can't talk," Jenny Lee whispered in a rush. "There's a rule about personal phone calls. For all I know, they listen in."

That gave Amanda pause, but she decided to risk it.

"This is business," she said briskly. She was more worried by the unexpected tension in Jenny Lee's voice and frustrated because she couldn't ask about it, than she was about the danger of having her end of the conversation overheard. "I want you to check around and see if either Sunland Electronics or Calvin Jones has outstanding loans there, business accounts, anything. Can you do it?"

"I'll be happy to do that for you, ma'am," Jenny Lee said with distant politeness.

"Thanks. Call me later."

"Will do."

"Jenny Lee?"

"Yes."

"Be careful."

"I'll be certain to do that," she said and hung up.

Whatever was going on at that bank, Amanda had a feeling that Ms. Van Sant was not going to win any awards as employer of the year. As soon as she'd hung up, Amanda grabbed her purse and headed for Sunland Electronics. Judging from the address, it was located in a warehouse area along the highway that stretched into Gwinnett County.

Sunland's two-story building was wedged in among other small businesses, body shops, and self-storage warehouses. The brick facade looked thoroughly out of place amid all that aluminum siding, as if it had been put there to prove that Sunland was a step above its neighbors.

Parking along the street was at a premium. The tiny Sunland lot was protected by a high fence topped by barbed wire. An out-of-shape security guard, who looked to be in his midforties, sat under an umbrella at the locked gate. When Amanda tooted her horn, he ambled over, hitching his pants over his belly as he walked.

"I'm here to see Mr. Jones. Can I park in the lot?"

"Afraid not. Employees only."

"What about visitors?"

"Don't have many."

"Where do you suggest I park?"

"Drive along the road here and keep your eyes open. Should be a spot someplace."

"Remind me to mention to the public relations people how helpful you were," Amanda said sarcastically. The comment clearly went over his head. Or through it.

"She found a parking place a block away in front of a trophy shop. She ignored the VIOLATORS WILL BE TOWED sign and pulled in. If they hauled her car away, Oscar could pay for it.

Irritated, she trampled back to Sunland and entered the lobby. The welcome mat didn't appear to be out in here either. A guard who looked like an elderly version of the one in the parking lot sat stoically on a straight-backed chair by a door that was bolted shut. There wasn't even a potted plant to cheer the place up. A fly buzzed around, looking futilely for someplace to land. Swatter in hand, the guard waited expectantly for it to do just that.

Amanda hated to intrude on their game, but she didn't want to spend a second longer in this dreary place than necessary. She glanced at the release Jack Davis had given her. "I'm here to see your public relations person. Mr. Wilson."

The guard glanced up at her. "Ain't here."

"Now or ever?"

"Left about six weeks ago."

"Who replaced him?"

"Nobody, so far's I know."

Amanda decided to go straight for the big time. "Mr. Jones, then."

He shrugged. "I'll try." He picked up the wall phone and punched in a number. "What's your name?"

"Amanda Roberts, *Inside Atlanta*."

He repeated it into the phone, listened, then nodded. He hung up, his expression giving away nothing. "Mr. Jones is unavailable."

"When will he be available?"

"Didn't say."

"Today? Tomorrow? Next year?"

He shrugged. "Didn't say."

Thoroughly exasperated, Amanda went down the block to the trophy shop and went inside. A young kid with all-American freckles and dirty blond hair looked up from an old issue of *Mad* magazine. Amanda smiled at him. He regarded her indifferently.

"I'm sorry to bother you, but could I use your phone? I just drove all the way out here from Atlanta and I need to check on an appointment nearby, but I can't find a pay phone."

He waved toward the old-fashioned black phone on a corner of the counter. "Help yourself."

Amanda dialed the number for Sunland that was on the press release and asked for Mr. Jones's office. His secretary picked up at once. At least she was efficient.

"Mr. Jones, please. I'm calling from the National Bank of the Netherlands," she said, counting on the gut instinct that told her that she'd hit pay dirt the first time out and that there was a link between Sunland and the bank.

"Certainly," she said, her entire manner suddenly very accommodating. "He's down the hall but I'll get him for you, if you don't mind waiting."

"I don't mind," Amanda said.

It took less than five minutes for Ms. Efficiency to retrieve her boss. When Calvin Jones picked up, he sounded breathless. Apparently any call from the bank was regarded as urgent.

"Mr. Jones, this is Amanda Roberts."

"Who? I thought this was Ms. Van Sant's office."

"Sorry. That was the only way I could get past your security system. I need to speak with you about a contract you got about six months ago."

Dead silence greeted her request. Then, sounding resigned, he asked, "How soon can you be here?"

"Five minutes. I'm just down the block."

"Fine," he said.

This time the guard in the lobby merely waved her into a long, dimly lit corridor. Entering it was a little like driving into an unfamiliar tunnel with no idea how far it was to the exit. It wasn't until she was halfway down that she saw an open door on the right, leading to a stairwell. She climbed to the second floor and stepped into another corridor that was a duplicate of the one downstairs except for a door all the way at the other end. Glancing in, she saw a secretary.

"I'm looking for Mr. Jones's office."

The chubby woman, who was wearing an unfortunate shade of yellow that turned her skin sallow, gave her a disgruntled look that said she didn't appreciate being lied to, then gestured toward the door. "Go on in. He's expecting you."

Calvin Jones rose when Amanda walked in. She couldn't be absolutely certain whether he'd done it out of politeness or to show off the fact that he was six-four and carried enough muscle to smash her like the fly that had been buzzing around the lobby. Either way, Amanda was impressed.

When she'd been seated in the office's one guest chair, he settled on a corner of his desk. In anyone else the choice might have implied informality. She had a feeling that Calvin Jones knew he was more imposing that way.

"So, Ms. Roberts, what's your interest in Sunland?" he asked, his expression merely curious. If he was worried by the visit, he wasn't going to let her see it.

Amanda considered how best to get into this. "I

understand that Sunland was having some financial difficulties a few months back.''

"I believe that was fairly widely reported at the time," he agreed. "It's old news."

"Your financial picture has stabilized?"

"Yes."

"How were you able to turn it around?" she asked, hoping he would leap to the conclusion that she was reporting on small businesses that had survived the tough economic times.

"I worked my butt off, Ms. Roberts. Sunland isn't just a business to me. It's proof that I'm a survivor. If you've done your homework, you know that I've overcome a few adversities in my time. I wasn't about to let money problems ruin what I've achieved."

"I can appreciate that," she said. "Could you be more specific about what steps you took?"

"Same things any other executive would do. I went after new business. Luckily, a major contract came through."

"With?"

He shook his head. "Sorry. That's something I can't get into."

"Merrill Hudson, by any chance?" she said, mentioning the name of the company that had been on that press release.

Alarm flared in his eyes, but he kept his voice even. "I can't get into the details. I'm sorry."

Amanda decided to sidestep that for the moment. "How'd you finance setting up for a major contract, especially if you were already having a rough time making it?"

"The same way any other business does, by taking that contract to the bank and proving that there would be sufficient income to cover the expenses and then some.''

"The National Bank of the Netherlands?''

His impassive expression never faltered. "I didn't say that.''

"No,'' she said. "You didn't. But I'm right, aren't I? Mentioning that bank was the only thing that got you on the phone earlier, after I'd been told not five minutes before that you were unavailable.''

He refused to be baited. "No businessman ever turns down a call from a financial institution. Those kinds of contacts always come in handy.''

"I can always check with the bank to see if you have loans there.''

He smiled at that. "Can you really?'' he said doubtfully.

"A credit check would do it, too,'' she assured him. "It's not the kind of thing you can hide.''

The smile widened. "I'll take my chances.'' He stood up. "If that's all...''

Amanda stood. It hardly made her an even match for him, but it did improve the subtle dynamics. "One last question. Where are you shipping the equipment you're manufacturing for Merrill Hudson?''

"I ship it to Buffalo,'' he said easily. "That's where their headquarters is.''

So, Amanda thought as she left, Sunland was covered should anyone discover any illegalities about the final destination of this equipment. Shipping it to Buffalo violated nothing.

But exactly where, she wondered, did it go from Buffalo?

# CHAPTER

## *Thirteen*

SO far Amanda had come up with three links in the complicated daisy chain, not nearly enough to make it stretch to Washington. The fact that the FBI seemed to have a certain fascination with her investigation wasn't proof of much. Maybe they were just hoping she'd do their legwork for them. Again. The thought made her want to chuck the whole investigation. Unfortunately, she was already hooked. She could hardly wait to find the rest of the links.

Rather than heading straight back into Atlanta, though, she stopped at a fast food restaurant for some cholesterol and contemplation. Over french fries and a hamburger, she considered the implications of what she'd learned from Calvin Jones.

It was possible that his deal with Merrill Hudson was totally on the up and up. But his evasiveness, combined with that link to the National Bank of the Netherlands, made her wonder. If she could confirm that his loans had been secured by that bank, it would be a start. Maybe Jenny Lee would come up with something by tonight.

In the meantime, she could check in to Merrill Hudson. She would rather do it in person, but Oscar would never okay a trip to Buffalo on the heels of that trip to Virginia. Not unless she had positive proof that it would tie together all the loose ends of the story. So far that wasn't the case. She could very well be heading down a blind alley.

Still munching on her french fries, she found a pay phone outside near the kiddie playground and called her mother at the office.

"Would you look up a company called Merrill Hudson for me?" she said, practically shouting over the noise of half a dozen toddlers squealing as they shot down the bright yellow slide and climbed through the huge red mouth of a gigantic plastic clown. "Check the data base in the computer first. Then go to the library if you have to."

"What am I looking for?"

"I'm not sure. Get me a list of corporate officers. Where they do business. Major deals. Any government contracts. How they're financed. Anything at all that seems suspicious."

"I'll start right away. By the way, Jenny Lee called back a few minutes ago. She says she couldn't find any account for Sunland Electronics or Calvin Jones. She also says there's something funny with the bank's computer system."

"Funny how?"

"She said when she tried to call up records for Sunland, it didn't just indicate that there was no such account or that there was an error. She had the feeling that there might be files requiring a different password than the one she'd been given.''

"Did she try entering something she knew was wrong to see what sort of signal she got?''

Her mother chuckled. ''You two definitely think alike. She did. She entered *Inside Atlanta* because she knew there was no account and she entered her own name. The computer said flatly that no such files existed.''

"A second set of records,'' Amanda said.

"That's what I thought, too,'' her mother agreed. ''Jenny Lee's going to snoop around if she can and see if there's some way to break the code.''

Amanda wondered if Richard Howell hadn't found that code, either at work or by hacking from home. It was possible that he would have written it down and hidden it somewhere in his home office. She put another visit to the house high on her list of things to do. Maybe she'd even ask Jim Harrison to get her inside. Going through the front door would be a pleasant change.

"You had another call,'' her mother said.

"From?''

"A man. He sounded French. He didn't want to leave his name. You don't suppose it was that arms dealer? You never said how that meeting went.''

"It was . . .'' She hesitated, choosing her words carefully. ''Interesting.''

Her mother pounced on the reaction with years worth of maternal instinct. ''Amanda, I don't like the sound of that.''

"I said it was interesting, for goodness' sake.''

"It was your tone of voice. It was the same tone you get whenever you're intrigued with someone.''

"He's an international arms dealer,'' she retorted

defensively. "Why wouldn't I be intrigued? Professionally speaking, that is. Besides, the man had me followed."

"What! Are you sure?" There was no mistaking her mother's alarm over that.

"I'm sure. The guy tailed me all the way to Dulles Airport. He disappeared right after I was shot at," she said without thinking.

"Oh, dear Lord. Amanda, why didn't you say something last night? Were you hurt?"

"Just a nick from some flying glass. You've seen me, Mother. I didn't look mortally wounded, did I?"

"No, but shouldn't you tell the police or the FBI or somebody?"

"You have to be kidding."

"Oscar then?"

"I don't think so. He'll just go all paternalistic on me and want to call in Donelli."

"I suppose you're right," her mother said with obvious reluctance. "But be careful, darling."

"I am always careful, Mother."

Apparently not careful enough, however. As she drove out of the parking lot, she noticed a familiar red sports car slipping into traffic right behind her. Surely it was coincidence, she thought. She'd just been talking about Armand LeConte's watchdog and now she was imagining him. There were probably hundreds of cars just like his in Atlanta.

Those were all perfectly rational arguments, but she couldn't deny the sudden edginess stealing through her. She slowed until the car either had to ride on her back bumper or pass. It passed. When it did, she caught sight of the Virginia license plates. That went beyond coincidence.

"Well, hell," she muttered. Without signaling, she

swerved to the shoulder of the road and stopped. She waited for a good ten minutes to see if the driver would circle back. He didn't.

Unfortunately, when she drove on, she'd barely crested the next hill before spotting him on the side of the road up ahead. He pulled neatly into traffic behind her again, apparently unconcerned at being detected. The audacity infuriated her almost as much as his presence.

The instant Amanda reached her office, she grabbed up a phone and punched in LeConte's number. Apparently her annoyance was clear to the man who'd answered. LeConte was on the line before she could say Uzi.

"*Ma chérie*, it is good to hear from you again," he said in a low murmur probably meant to trip her heartstrings.

"Call him off," she said bluntly, determinedly ignoring the expected leap of her pulse.

"Pardon?"

"Your pal with the red sports car. Call him off."

"I do not think that would be wise."

She noticed he didn't waste time denying the man's existence. "What's he after?"

"He is not *after* anything, *ma chérie*. He is there for your own protection."

"My protection! Mr. LeConte . . ."

"Armand."

"Mr. LeConte," she said adamantly. "I do not require protection. Yours or anyone else's."

"I think perhaps I am a better judge of that than you. You seem to be, shall we say, somewhat impetuous. Do you not realize that someone shot at you yesterday shortly after you left my home? It was most fortunate that I had the foresight to send Henri after you."

"For all I know it was your pal who fired that shot."

"I assure you, he did not. You needn't worry about that particular gentleman again, however. His recovery will be slow."

He sounded grim. More frightening to Amanda, he sounded pleased.

"My God," she said, sinking into a chair. "What happened to him?"

"He suffered an unfortunate accident," he said matter-of-factly. "You can see, then, why I feel it necessary to keep an eye on you."

"I am not your responsibility," she repeated, aware that she was wasting her breath. Maybe she'd display a little Southern hospitality and invite her unwanted body-guard over for tea. That ought to disconcert him. Maybe he knew secrets about his boss that he'd like to share, leverage she could use the next time they had one of these no-win conversations.

"By the way," she began, shifting gears, "tell me about Merrill Hudson."

"This is a person?" he inquired after an unmistakable beat.

"You'll have to be quicker than that, Mr. LeConte. You know perfectly well it is not. It's a company in Buffalo."

"He sighed. "*Merde*. You will be a trial for me, will you not, Amanda?"

"If possible," she confirmed cheerfully. "You were about to tell me about Merrill Hudson."

"No, *ma chérie*, I was not."

"*Au revoir*, then. I've got work to do. Just so you know, if you genuinely want me out of danger, the sooner I get the information I need, the better."

"Amanda!"

She hung up on him. To her deep regret, she found that she had done it with some reluctance.

When she looked up, she saw her mother regarding her quizzically. "That was him, wasn't it?"

"Him who?"

"That arms dealer."

"Yes. I called to tell him to call off the man he has following me. It wasn't enough that he had me tailed to the airport. He sent the guy all the way to Atlanta."

Instead of looking indignant or even alarmed, her mother suddenly smiled. "I think that's rather sweet."

"It is not *sweet*," Amanda said through gritted teeth.

"Is he going to call the man off?"

"No. He refused. He thinks he's being helpful," she said, then pointedly changed the subject. "What did you find out about Merrill Hudson?"

Still looking amused, her mother handed her a stack of computer printouts.

"I'll go through these later," Amanda said, putting them aside. "Fill me in."

"The U.S. headquarters are in Buffalo. The company's main office is in Amsterdam. The president, Graham Hudson, whose father founded the company with Laurence Merrill, is a disenchanted American ex-patriate. Apparently he's willing to sell anything to the highest bidder. He skirts U.S. law by making legitimate deals in this country, then sending the high-tech equipment to his overseas headquarters before passing it on to his international customers. He always claims he is unaware of any military use the equipment might have. In at least a dozen stories I found, he purports to be 'a simple businessman, a mere go-between.'"

"Sounds just like LeConte."

"Let that be a warning to you, dear."

"Not two minutes ago, you thought he was being sweet."

"Appreciating his little kindness is not the same as cozying up to him," her mother retorted.

Amanda scowled at her. She thought calling an unwanted bodyguard who dispatched people "a little kindness" was like suggesting that murder was a small indiscretion. However, it was not something that she cared to debate at the moment. "What will it take to stop Hudson?" she wondered. "Will they have to catch him hooking this stuff up to a nuclear missile?"

"That would be the easy way," her mother agreed.

"I don't understand something, though. If it's that well documented that he's trading in high-tech machinery that's winding up in the hands of the enemy, how does he continue to get permission to ship it out of the country? Doesn't the State Department or somebody have to give the go-ahead for this stuff to leave the U.S.?"

"Obviously somebody is turning a blind eye, either on his own or because someone higher up has told him to. If I understand the system, an inspector merely has to apply the least stringent evaluation of the equipment's purpose and off it goes," her mother said.

"Then all I have to do is figure out who's doing the inspecting or who's telling them to go easy, and then prove it."

Jeffrey Dunne's reaction from the outset of this investigation suggested he knew more than he was saying about who that someone might be. Amanda debated trying one more time to get him to give her a straight answer. Maybe if she indulged in a little conjecture, his expression alone would tell her if she was getting close to the truth.

She was about to call and arrange a meeting when the

phone rang. She grabbed it. "Amanda Roberts."

"I was beginning to think you'd taken off for a Club Med vacation," Jim Harrison said.

"Why on earth would you think that?"

"You haven't been dogging me with questions for more than twenty-four hours."

"True," she said, chuckling. "I thought I'd give you time to catch up with me."

"Very funny."

"I assume you didn't call just to yank my chain. What's up?"

"I thought you ought to know that the Richard Howell case has been ever-so-gently removed from my jurisdiction. Not that there is an official case," he amended. "No body. No hard evidence of foul play. Even so, somebody cares enough to put it in the hands of the very best."

Amanda drew in a deep breath. Although he sounded reasonably calm, she knew how deeply such power plays infuriated him. "Anybody say why?"

"No. They didn't feel the need to share that information with me. They never do," he said bitterly. "As a parting gesture, I thought perhaps I would offer you my copy of the key to Howell's house, even though I know you're perfectly capable of climbing through windows. If you have any desire to take another look around, I suggest you do it before the FBI swarms all over the place."

"How long do I have?"

"I thought I might meander over there and turn over the files later this afternoon. Let Dunne cool his heels for a change."

Amanda grabbed her purse. "I'll meet you at the house in twenty minutes."

She made it there in fifteen. Harrison was waiting for her out front.

"I said twenty minutes," she reminded him. "You're early."

"It's a twenty-minute drive only if you obey the speed limit, Amanda. You never do." He handed her the key. "You're on your own. If you ever tell a living, breathing soul where you got this key, I will have a policeman on your back bumper from dawn to dusk. You'll have to ride MARTA if you want to get anywhere in a hurry."

"I just love inventive police harassment."

His grin was unrepentant. "I thought you might."

"Sure you don't want to come inside with me?"

"Amanda, I'm angry, not professionally suicidal."

"Okay," she said, as he shoved his hands in his pockets and started away. "Hey, Harrison."

He glanced back.

"I'll let you know what I find."

"Can you think of any other reason I'd give you the key?"

Amanda didn't waste another minute before getting inside and going straight back to Richard Howell's den. Though the original police search had been less careful than her own, the room was essentially orderly. Apparently they hadn't seen a need to toss the place, probably because they hadn't had a clue about what they were looking for.

She began with the computer, lifting each piece to see if he'd stuck the bank's code word underneath. Then she checked the insides of the drawers, the bottom of the trashcan, and along the underside of the desk itself. Nothing. She turned over the phone to check the base. Zero.

She paced the room again, looking for some other

hiding place, some hint of what he might have done with the information he had, even a clue about why he'd come to her in the first place. Why not a reporter on the *Constitution*? He'd mentioned knowing that she tended to take risks. How?

She fingered the collection of sci-fi books, praying that he hadn't tucked the information into one of those. Just in case, she looked at the titles to see if any linked in any way, even remotely, to banking. At the end of a row, she noticed a stack of magazines she'd missed on the earlier visit. All editions of *Inside Atlanta*, going back to the premiere issue. In each one there were pages marked, all for her stories. So, then, he had followed her Atlanta career, had somehow surmised from her reporting that she would take a crack at a complicated, dangerous story with little hard evidence to lure her in. That still didn't tell her a damned thing, though, about this case.

Frustrated, she sat back down and tried to put herself into Richard Howell's head. Where would he have hidden a password? Where would a hacker put something for safekeeping?

In his own computer files, of course. Amanda turned on the computer and waited for it to boot up. That much was simple enough. Unfortunately, if he'd done anything terribly complicated to keep his secret, she was up a creek. Beyond writing her stories and utilizing certain data bases, computers were essentially a mystery to her. She might not be a computer illiterate, but she was only one step removed.

Aware of the fact that the FBI could show up at any moment, even without Jim Harrison's keys and files, Amanda glanced at the directory and felt a momentary flurry of panic. There was no way she could open all those files and read through them. Nor was there time to print them out. There was, however, time to copy them all onto disks so that someone else could look through them at their leisure.

She spotted a box of blank diskettes, popped one into place, and began copying anything that looked as if it might have any relevance to Richard Howell's work. Only when she'd been at it for well over two hours did she begin to realize that the files on his extensive hard disk were seemingly endless. Still, she kept on.

She'd worked her way through three-fourths of the files before she came to one labeled *Roberts*. She couldn't resist the temptation to call it up then and there. Surely the name of the file wasn't mere coincidence.

"I knew you'd find this sooner or later, Amanda," it began. "I hope you broke into the house to get it. That would confirm what I thought I knew about you. You're the kind of reporter who won't let this story die."

Amanda was flattered, but she wished he'd get to the point. Every creak in this old house made the hairs on the back of her neck stand up.

"I hope you know someone who knows their way around a computer. Otherwise the password from the bank won't do you any good. I can't imagine Ms. Van Sant welcoming you in to poke around in her files. You'll either have to get someone inside or find a hacker with a modem and the ability to break through security codes for the bank itself."

Since it appeared that Richard wasn't going to give her those bank security codes, Amanda was incredibly grateful that they'd been able to get Jenny Lee inside that bank. Even there, she might not have access to any deeply hidden records, password or not. She read on.

"Once you've accessed the computer," he wrote,

"the word you need to get to that second set of bank records is *bitte*, the German for *please*. Nice touch, don't you think?"

*A little too cute for words*, Amanda thought.

"Anyway," he continued, "you should find everything you need in those files to prove that the bank is underwriting loans that are covering equipment that ends up in Iraqi hands. I don't think the people overseas know about this. Our Ms. Van Sant is greedy and ambitious. Somebody here in town lured her into this deal. She's pretty chummy with some heavy hitters. I'm almost certain she's getting a healthy cut of whatever the loan amount is. Couldn't check that, though. She doesn't keep her money in our bank. My guess would be the Caymans. If you're reading this, something's probably happened to me. I sure wish I could have been around for the finale. Hope it's Pulitzer Prize caliber. Good luck. Richard."

Amanda sat staring at the screen, her eyes stinging with unexpected tears. Suddenly she wished she'd known Richard Howell. He had the same sort of spunk people were always crediting her with having. She had a feeling he'd gotten in the middle of this partly from idealism, partly out of a sense of adventure. Obviously he'd realized what sort of danger was involved. He could have walked away, but he hadn't. Once again, she resolved to tie all the pieces together and make those responsible pay, not only for their international crimes but for Richard's death.

She did a quick printout of the letter, then erased it from the computer files. If anyone else started checking through these directories, she didn't want them to find that letter. She tucked her copy into her purse.

On her way out of the house, Amanda took a quick

look around the living room, hoping to find a photo of Richard Howell that she could eventually use with her story. She found a family album in the drawer of an end table. She flipped it open and thumbed through the pages hurriedly until she found a picture of a young man she could say for certain was her confidential informant that night in the cemetery. She didn't waste time glancing through the rest of the pictures. She tucked the entire album under her arm and slipped out the front door, locking it carefully behind her.

On her way back to the office, she put in a call to Larry Carter, knowing he'd be in front of the TV watching the Braves as they made a bid to win the National League championship. There wasn't a photography assignment on the face of the earth that could have lured him away from that game.

"Hey, Larry, what's the score?"

"The Braves are up by one in the eighth, but Pittsburgh has two men on base, two outs. Talk fast."

"I need you to call your friend in the photo department at the *Journal-Constitution*. I need to have him check their files to see if a banker named Van Sant has been photographed in the past year or so."

"You looking for a head shot or what?"

"I'm hoping she'll be in a group picture with somebody important. I'd be thrilled with the President. I'll settle for a senator, even the mayor."

"You have a first name?"

"Helga."

"Got it. Where will you be?"

"I'm on my way back to the office now," she said, just as she heard a roar from the crowd on Larry's TV. He never even said goodbye, just whooped as the phone clicked in her ear. The Braves must have gotten that third Pirate out.

# CHAPTER

## *Fourteen*

IT was nearly eight when Amanda returned to the office. Most of the staff had gone long ago, but she found Jenny Lee there with her mother. Both of them looked exhausted.

"How'd it go today?" Amanda asked. The two women exchanged a look she couldn't read. She had a feeling, though, that they'd been conspiring. It was a disconcerting thought.

"Food," Jenny Lee cried weakly. "You get nothing from me until you feed me."

Amanda glanced at her mother.

"I'm afraid that goes for me too, dear," she said. "The only thing I've had all day was a package of stale peanut butter crackers from that vending machine down the hall." She shuddered dramatically. "Those things ought to be outlawed. I spoke with Oscar about it. I told him things would be much more efficient around here if there was a nice coffee shop on the premises.''

"How did he react to that?''

"He told me he'd take it under advisement.'' She regarded Amanda with some skepticism. "I was thinking of giving him a written proposal tomorrow, so he won't forget. What do you think?''

"I'm sure he'll love that,'' Amanda said dryly. "I assume from this pathetic display that neither of you will settle for anything less than a decent meal at a nice restaurant. No take-out sandwiches from the deli down the street?''

"Steak,'' Jenny Lee concurred.

"Grilled chicken or fish,'' her mother countered sternly, having learned her dietary lessons at numerous expensive spas. "Maybe pasta.''

"Let's go, then. I never thought I'd see the day when I had to bribe my own assistants into turning over the information they'd gathered.''

"Face it, Amanda. Around here, you never even thought you'd have assistants,'' Jenny Lee shot back. "Count your blessings.''

Her spirits had evidently improved considerably now that dinner was in the offing . . . even if the menu wasn't likely to include beef as long as she was in Elisa Bailey's forceful presence.

To Amanda's amusement Jenny Lee continued to hold out until they were actually seated in a restaurant overlooking downtown Atlanta. Looking awestruck, Jenny Lee gazed around at the panoramic view.

"Wow! I never thought you'd spring for this place.''

"I'm not,'' Amanda said. "Oscar is. We're here to talk business. Enjoy yourselves.''

She listened as Jenny Lee and her mother dissected

the menu with the enthusiasm of two gourmets given carte blanche to sample the wares in a five-star kitchen. After stylishly preparing the food for dozens of elegant dinner parties, Elisa Bailey could probably match the Cordon Bleu chef here entrée for entrée. Amanda was delighted to see her once again contemplating with enthusiasm something more substantial than tea. It was yet more proof that hard work could at least temporarily take a person's mind off their troubles.

When the orders were in and the waiter had poured them each a glass of California chardonnay, Amanda regarded them pointedly. "Okay, let's hear it. If I'm going to explain away the cost of this meal, it had better be good."

Jenny Lee had just opened her mouth to reply, when she suddenly turned pale as a ghost. "I think I'd better leave," she said in a rush, ducking down as if she were picking something up off the floor.

Amanda glanced down at her blankly. "Why? You were the one who was starving."

"Over there," Jenny Lee replied, pointing nervously across the dining room.

Amanda followed the direction of her gesture and saw Ms. Helga Van Sant just sitting down. Although she was being seated at a cozy table for four, she was alone.

"She can't see me with you," Jenny Lee said miserably. "It'll ruin everything."

"Go," Amanda agreed. "I'll stop by the table and keep her attention focused on me until you can get out of here."

"My dinner," Jenny Lee said plaintively.

"We'll have them box it up and bring it back to the

office. Wait for us there. Larry's supposed to call or stop by there anyway.''

The prospect of talking to Larry cheered her considerably. Jenny Lee was still trying to convince the photographer that getting married would not ruin their wonderful relationship. Larry claimed to love her, but he had his doubts. Personally, Amanda thought it had something to do with the fact that Jenny Lee didn't share his appreciation for the Braves. Every game they went to, she cheered for the opposing team.

"Hurry," Jenny Lee said. "I can't stay down here like this forever. People are already starting to stare."

"How can you tell from that angle? All you can see are their feet," Amanda countered.

"Just go," Jenny Lee pleaded.

Amanda crossed the room to Ms. Van Sant's table. Without asking permission, she pulled out a chair and took a seat opposite the banker. "Hello again," she said cheerfully.

The banker didn't bat an eye at the intrusion. "Ms. Roberts, isn't it?" she said pleasantly. "Have you been able to locate our Mr. Howell yet?"

"Not yet," Amanda said. "But I will. I gather you haven't had any word either."

"No, I'm sorry to say. Such a bright young man. I truly thought he had an outstanding future with us." She shook her head sadly.

"Ms. Van Sant, I was wondering, how would a person in your position go about hiding loans she didn't want on the official bank records?"

Though her expression remained impassive, her gaze narrowed almost imperceptibly. "I beg your pardon."

"Theoretically speaking, of course," Amanda assured her blithely. "It's just something I've been wondering about ever since that scandal with the Banca Nazionale. How could that manager have gotten away with it for so long without anyone else in the bank catching on?"

"I'm sure I have no idea," she said, any hint of warmth stripped from her voice. "Really, Ms. Roberts, I am expecting someone. If you don't mind . . ."

Amanda refused to acknowledge the blatant dismissal. "Surely, you and your peers must have speculated about such a thing," she persisted.

"We did not," Ms. Van Sant insisted. "Banking fraud is appalling enough without wallowing in the details over drinks like a bunch of old gossips. Now I must ask you to leave. Otherwise I shall be forced to go myself. I came here for a pleasant dinner, not an interrogation."

Since Amanda dearly wanted to see with whom Ms. Van Sant was dining, she stood up. "I'm sorry if my questions disturbed you," she apologized, with little sincerity in her tone. "My curiosity gets out of hand sometimes."

"I am not disturbed. I just find the questions tiresome," the banker countered, clearly hoping to convey that she had not been either evasive or fearful.

"Whatever," Amanda said politely. She nodded and went back to her own table.

Ms. Van Sant sat perfectly still for about sixty seconds, then got up, murmured a few words to the waiter, and headed for the door. Amanda followed, pausing to speak to the waiter.

"Excuse me. Did Ms. Van Sant happen to leave any message for her dinner companion?"

"Yes, miss. She asked that I tell him she had to take care of an emergency."

"And the gentleman's name?"

"Jones, miss."

Amanda had to hide a triumphant smile. "Thank you."

She walked back to her table. "It seems Ms. Van Sant was planning to dine with the president of Sunland Electronics, until I spoiled her appetite," she told her mother.

The links in that daisy chain were getting stronger all the time.

Jenny Lee's trout amandine looked a little the worse for wear by the time Amanda got it back to the *Inside Atlanta* office. It didn't seem to matter. Jenny Lee was munching dispiritedly on a package of peanut butter crackers. She took one look at the take-out container and grabbed for it.

"Has Larry called?" Amanda asked, holding the Styrofoam box aloft.

"About a half-hour ago. He's on his way in. He's gonna stop by the *Constitution* to pick up a couple of pictures he said you wanted."

"Did he tell you anything about them?"

"Nope. I'm not even sure he knew any details. The photographer over there just told him he'd pull some negatives and make prints for him. He said Ms. Van Sant turns up on the society pages all the time."

Just as Jenny Lee finished her explanation, and Amanda turned her dinner over to her, Larry came in. The photographer was whistling cheerfully and looking about as innocent as a kid trying to keep a family secret from a nosy neighbor.

With his shock of blond hair and freckles and his penchant for outrageous print shirts and jeans, Larry would always look like an overgrown kid. He was still one of the most talented and least ambitious photographers Amanda had ever run across. That was probably why any other photographer in town would do him a favor.

"Okay, what's the deal?" she demanded.

"The Braves won," he said, deliberately misunderstanding her meaning.

"Is that the only reason you're so cheerful?"

"It's a good enough reason for me."

"Larry!"

Ignoring her impatience, he deliberately turned and introduced himself to her mother. "Jenny Lee told me you were in town. How do you like it?"

"I'm having the time of my life," she said.

The comment was so remarkable, Amanda almost forgot to pester Larry. Almost. "Okay, okay. You've got the pleasantries out of the way. Let's hear about the pictures. Better yet, let's see them."

He grinned. "Settle down, Amanda. I have a feeling these are just what you had in mind."

He spread a half-dozen black and white photos across her desk. Helga Van Sant was in each, usually among three or four local society bigwigs, prominent businessmen, and their wives. Proof that she hobnobbed with an elite crowd, but nothing especially controversial. Unfortunately Calvin Jones wasn't one of those businessmen.

Amanda perused those disappointing shots one more time just to be sure there were no obvious links to her story, then she glanced up and caught the devilish gleam in Larry's eyes.

"Best for last," he told her and added one more. There, her arm linked through his, were Helga Van

Sant and Georgia's senior senator, a member of the Senate Foreign Relations Committee and a man whose violent anti-Iraqi rhetoric had helped to carry the Congress when the President sought approval for the Persian Gulf War and subsequent military presence in the Middle East.

"Fascinating, huh?" Larry said. "Jenny Lee filled me in on what you're working on. Explain to me what a woman with apparent ties to the Iraqi military would be doing arm in arm with Senator Blaine Rawlings?"

Amanda had a feeling that if she could explain that, she would be 90 percent of the way to her Pulitzer.

# CHAPTER

## *Fifteen*

SENATOR Blaine Rawlings played politics the way a New Orleans jazz musician slid over the low notes: slow and easy. Nothing pleased the 67-year-old, white-haired politician more than a lazy Sunday afternoon of barbecued ribs and corn on the cob, a few hours of kissing babies and making political small talk.

Longevity had made him one of the most powerful men on Capitol Hill. A charter member of the old boys' network in Georgia and in Washington, he didn't quite get the fact that today's electorate expected substance over style. To his consternation, a generally dissatisfied public, tired of ribs and inconsequential talk, had put his tenure in jeopardy. Of late he'd found himself fending off attacks from all angles. Publicly at least, he'd taken it in stride, dismissing the critics as opportunists and inexperienced rascals. His staff thought otherwise. Despite the widely reported confusion and anxiety among his strategists, Amanda found the senator at his family estate outside of Atlanta calmly cutting back a bed of rose bushes, unperturbed by all the commotion.

Red suspenders held up his khaki pants, giving him a jaunty look. A wide-brimmed straw hat shaded his eyes. He barely gave Amanda a glance when she strolled across the lawn.

"I'm sorry to bother you at home," she apologized. "But your office wasn't sure when you were expected."

"Keeps 'em on their toes," he said as he snipped off another stem. He squinted at her from under the brim of that hat. "Who're you?"

"Amanda Roberts, sir. I'm with *Inside Atlanta* magazine."

"Did we have an appointment?" he asked in a tone that implied an apology, even while suggesting that he knew perfectly well one wasn't called for.

"No. I just took a chance on finding you here."

"Enterprising," he said approvingly. "I could use somebody like that. You after a job?"

"No. I have a job."

"That don't mean you wouldn't like a better one."

"True, but I happen to like the one I have."

He pulled a huge white handkerchief out of his back pocket and mopped his brow. "How about a glass of lemonade? It's hotter than Hades out here today. You'd never guess it was moving on toward November. Maybe there's something to that global-warming hogwash."

As impatient as she was, Amanda figured she'd stand a much better chance of getting the information she was after if she followed his agenda. "Lemonade would be nice."

"You go inside and tell Velma, if you don't mind. I'll just finish here and we can sit in the shade and enjoy ourselves. It's been a long time since a pretty young lady came to call," he said, the line sounding like something out of a Tennessee Williams play.

Amanda knew better than to take the shuffling, aw-shucks routine too seriously. If anything, the old man was simply sizing her up, trying to regain whatever control he might feel he'd lost when she had turned up out of the blue. More than one fellow Congressman had made the mistake of misjudging his intelligence and had paid dearly for it by being skewered publicly by a man who never misjudged his political enemies.

Inside the house Amanda found Velma in the kitchen. The housekeeper, a wiry, elderly black woman with sharp eyes and a tart tongue, shook her head when Amanda explained her mission.

"Don't that man know you ain't supposed to send a guest on errands? You go on out and sit in one of them chairs under that big old oak tree down by the creek. I'll be along in a minute. He'll be wanting some of my fresh-baked sugar cookies to go with that lemonade."

She gave Amanda a conspiratorial look. "Doctor told him to give up sugar a year ago or more, but he does have a sweet tooth. Always did. Won't let me use that substitute either. He can spot the difference with the first taste. Said he'd fire me on the spot if I tried fooling him again." She chuckled at the senator's stubbornness. "You go along now, child."

"I could take a tray back and save you the trip," Amanda offered.

"No, indeed. The senator might forget his manners, but I don't. You go right along. Just follow the path past the rose garden."

As she walked along the gravel path that wound along the eastern edge of the garden, Amanda noticed that the clippers and a pair of work gloves had been left on a white wrought iron bench. She followed the path and emerged on a shady stretch of lawn that edged up to a slow-moving creek. The senator was already seated in an old-fashioned wicker rocker. He glanced up.

"You find Velma okay?"

Amanda nodded and sat in the companion rocker, noting the portable phone on the table between them. She hadn't seen it earlier, but it was small enough to have been in his pocket. It was interesting that as relaxed as he had seemed in that rose garden, he'd never been out of touch with his office or anyone else who might need him in an emergency.

"She'll be down in a minute," she told him. "She's bringing cookies, too. They were just coming out of the oven when I left."

He nodded in satisfaction, then studied her thoughtfully. Finally, an amused twinkle in his eyes, he said, "You look like you're 'bout to bust a gusset, girl. Why don't you tell me what brings you here?"

"I'm working on a story. It's beginning to look as if it can be tracked all the way to Washington."

His humor faded as he pinned her with his shrewd blue eyes. "What sort of story?"

"The way it's shaping up, it looks to me as if some businesses here in Georgia are all mixed up with getting military technology to the Iraqis."

Not so much as an eyelash flickered. "Bull!" he said succinctly. "After that business with the Eye-talian bank, don't you think we'd be watching for that sort of thing?"

"I would have thought so," she agreed as Velma

arrived and deposited the tray of refreshments on the wicker table between them. There were frosty glasses of lemonade, a pitcher with extra, plus a plate of sugar cookies.

Amanda waited until the senator had served himself and was munching happily on a cookie before adding, "But the fact of the matter is, this *is* happening. I've traced the shipment of goods from here to Buffalo, from Buffalo to Amsterdam. From there they're going to Iraq. I'm convinced of it."

"You have proof?" he asked, wiping irritably at the cookie crumbs on his chest.

"Nothing I'm ready to print yet, but it's coming together bit by bit."

"Why are you coming to me with this?"

"Because last night I saw a picture of you taken with the banker who seems to be covering the loans for the Iraqis. Helga Van Sant."

Genuine astonishment spread across his face. "Helga? I don't believe it. Why, she and I go way back. I know her about as well as I know my own daughters."

"Which might make her the perfect person to slip something past you," Amanda suggested, waiting to see if he snatched at the easy out.

"Honey, I may be old and I know some folks think I'm a damn fool, but nobody slips anything past me unless I let 'em."

"If that's true and this is happening, then that must mean it's going on with your approval," Amanda countered. "You can't have it both ways, Senator."

"With all due respect, young lady, I only have your word that this is happening at all. I assume you won't take offense if I do a little checking around myself."

Amanda smiled. "I wish you would. In fact, I'd be

happy to dial Ms. Van Sant's number for you. I have it right here.'' She reached for the cellular phone on the table between them.

"I think maybe I'll just make those calls from inside. You want to wait here? Drink your lemonade. I'll be back in a bit.''

Amanda figured that staying right where she was wasn't altogether awful. If he wasn't involved and his calls confirmed her story, he might be outraged enough to share that information.

When he had gone, she slipped her shoes off and ran her toes through the cool grass, indulging in a little trip down memory lane. There had been plenty of afternoons just like this at her grandmother's house during her childhood. Lazy, sultry Indian summer days that cried out for a hammock and a good book. Closing her eyes and sipping her lemonade, Amanda was ten years old again and life was blissfully uncomplicated.

The low murmur of voices on the path snapped her back to the definitely complicated present. Two men in suits, looking as if they were sweltering in the unseasonal heat, were striding toward her.

"Ms. Roberts, we'd like you to come with us, please.''

As the implication of what they were asking sank in, she regarded them in astonishment. The old guy had turned her in, probably claiming she was some loony trespasser. "You're kidding, right?''

"I'm afraid not. We need to ask you some questions.''

"Have a seat,'' she suggested. "Ask away.''

"I think it would be better if you came along with us.''

It was only a guess, but Amanda was nearly 100 percent certain that these two didn't represent the local sheriff. His minions tended toward plaid shirts and baseball caps. "Come along where?"

"Atlanta."

"Could you be a little more precise? My mother always told me never to go anywhere with strangers."

"FBI headquarters, Ms. Roberts."

"ID, please," she said, holding out her hand and marveling at the senator's sneakiness. He'd left her here to her uncomplicated thoughts and gone inside to rat on her. Damn him.

Naturally the two men had identification galore and the stubborn determination to match.

"Fine," she said agreeably after surveying every last piece of ID. "I'll follow you back into town."

One of them actually cracked a smile at that. "Afraid not. I'll take your car. You can ride with Mills here."

She shrugged with feigned indifference. "Whatever. I hope you won't mind if we pass through the house. I'd like to say goodbye to the senator and thank him for his exceptional Southern hospitality."

"Not necessary. We'll tell him you sent your regards."

"Will you also tell him that this little stunt puts him into the middle of this scam right up to his eyeballs?" she said, trying to keep the fury out of her voice.

To her regret, they didn't stop long enough to pass along her message. She'd have to deliver it personally at some future date. She could always slip it to her first visitor at the federal penitentiary, which was where these two seemed inclined to send her.

Unfortunately Mills wasn't the talkative type. Maybe he figured since he hadn't informed her of her rights, they ought to keep conversation to a minimum.

"Am I under arrest?" she inquired. That's definitely

what it felt like, but no one had mentioned that nasty word so far.

He glanced over at her. "Should you be?"

"Not by my standards, but you guys play by your own rules."

He didn't comment on that observation. When she'd been escorted into FBI headquarters, she was trotted into an office and told to stay put. It was no surprise that the next person through the door was Jeffrey Dunne. He didn't seem overjoyed to see her.

"You had to keep pushing, didn't you?" he said ruefully.

"Just doing my job. This whole story gets curiouser and curiouser. What am I doing here?"

"The government and most especially the senior senator from Georgia are interested in knowing your source."

"You could have asked. You didn't have to send the troops out to drag me in."

"Okay," he said blandly. "Who's your source?"

"Sorry. Can't reveal it," she said. Even though Richard Howell was dead, he deserved her protection. "Whistleblowers are not popular in Washington."

"Then Washington should clean up its act," she retorted. "That would put them out of business."

Dunne looked as if he'd had a very bad day. "Amanda, I don't enjoy this."

"Sure you do. This is what you're trained for—hassling reporters and private citizens. It must give you quite a charge. It occurs to me, though, that you're poking around in the wrong places. I'm more fascinated with why someone is nervous enough to be killing over this story. I'm intrigued with why a United States senator would haul the FBI out to his home to pick up a reporter for asking a few innocent questions.''

"Innocent?''

"They were unless he had something to feel mighty guilty about. Remember those bad guys, Dunne? At the moment, it seems as if they are you, to paraphrase somebody or other. Now charge me with something or let me go.''

She was counting on the agent's innate sense of fair play to release her. He knew she wasn't guilty of a damn thing, and while he could hold her for not revealing her source, a decent lawyer would have her out on bail by nightfall. Besides, they both knew that the FBI already knew exactly who her source was. Otherwise Jim Harrison would still be working on the Howell murder case. This was just a ploy to harass her and it was making her very irritable.

"Get out of here, Amanda,'' he said wearily, just as Oscar came charging through the door with a look of outrage on his face.

"What the hell is going on here, Dunne?'' he said, stepping close until he was right in the agent's face.

Amanda tried to wedge herself between them. "It's okay, Oscar. He's just released me.''

Oscar took a step back, but he kept right on glaring. "Why the hell did he haul you in in the first place?''

"I'll explain later,'' she said, tugging him toward the door. The last thing she needed was for Oscar and Jeffrey Dunne to get into an altercation. The FBI was just looking for excuses to put people away today, it seemed.

Outside, her boss looked her up and down. "You okay?''

"Just peachy.''

"Take the rest of the day off. Take your mother with you," he suggested, a certain unmistakable, heartfelt edge to his voice.

"What's wrong? Didn't you like her proposal for a coffee shop?"

"Exactly how long is she planning to hang around?" he asked, ignoring her question.

Amanda wished she knew the answer to that. "Hard to say. Is she making you nervous?"

"She's back in the office preparing to call out the National Guard if you're not back there in the next thirty minutes. I think the stress is getting to her."

"How'd you find out about this anyway?"

"We got an anonymous tip. Some guy with a French accent. Your mother said something about the body-guard Armand LeConte had trailing you around. Would you care to explain what the hell that's all about?"

"You don't want to know," Amanda assured him. She would have to call the arms dealer and tell him that just this once she was grateful for his intervention. She hoped her gratitude wouldn't encourage him to make a practice of it.

Although she wanted nothing more than to get back to work, Amanda took one look at her mother's frantic expression and decided that Oscar was right. They'd both be better off at home.

As they made the long drive, Amanda couldn't help glancing in the rearview mirror every few seconds to assure herself that the red sports car was right behind. To her relief, it was. She didn't want the guy smushing her presumed enemies, but it wouldn't hurt to have him around as backup since it didn't seem she could count on the Establishment to be on her side lately.

When she turned into her driveway, the car followed

her, then pulled discreetly from view behind some shrubs. Her mother glanced over her shoulder and caught sight of the red bumper.

"That's him, isn't it? The bodyguard?"

"Yes."

She nodded in satisfaction. "Good."

"Mother, that bodyguard was sent here by an international arms dealer."

"Well, obviously he has more sense than some other people I could name," she said indignantly as she stepped out of the car.

Suddenly she paused and slid back inside. "Amanda, she whispered urgently.

Amanda glanced at her. "What?"

"Who is that absolutely gorgeous man sitting on your front porch?"

She followed the direction of her mother's gaze and sighed heavily. Her day had just plummeted from bad to worse.

"That," she said wearily, "is Armand LeConte."

# CHAPTER

## *Sixteen*

ARMAND LeConte looked about as out of place on Amanda's tiny front porch as a mountain lion would prowling around on the White House lawn. The only possible explanation for his presence made her very nervous.

"*Bonjour, ma chérie*," he said as casually as if he were always there to greet her after a hard day at the office.

All the while, his gaze caressed her, slowly and intently, as if he were looking for bruises or other outward signs of her ordeal at the hands of the FBI. That possessive, intimate examination confirmed her worst fears.

"You are okay?" he inquired, his gentle voice counterpointed by the fierce gleam in his eyes.

"No worse than I would be with a bad case of PMS," she muttered.

"Pardon?"

"Never mind."

"Amanda, dear, where are your manners?" her mother said, referring no doubt to the lack of an introduction, rather than her ill-considered remark about the state of her health.

Reluctantly Amanda performed the introductions. After whatever he might have done to see to Amanda's rescue this afternoon, her mother appeared willing to forgive Armand LeConte whatever indiscretions he'd engaged in on the international arms scene. If he'd parked a tank on the front lawn, she probably would have considered it as fitting a gift as a bouquet of roses.

While the two of them oozed charm, Amanda went inside and took two aspirin. Then she shrugged and took one more. She didn't have a headache at the moment, but she had a hunch she ought to plan ahead.

Then Armand stepped into the kitchen and the room seemed to shrink. He glanced around at the inexpensive furniture and the old fashioned appliances and smiled. "Charming, *ma chérie*. It suits you."

Since Amanda had always thought of herself as very modern, she wasn't quite sure how to take the comment. She settled for a simple nod of thanks.

"You have lived here for some time?"

"A few years now."

"And before that?"

"New York."

He fixed an intense, curious gaze on her. "Fascinating. This, I think, suits you more. Here you stand out, a bird of paradise among ordinary roses. In New York . . ."

His shoulders rose slightly in a very Gallic shrug. "Not so extraordinary."

Amanda decided she had never been insulted quite so beautifully. Of course, it was part of his charm that he considered the analysis of her life to be his business. He obviously had no idea how irritating she found it.

"Why are you here?" she grumbled impolitely.

"Because, *chérie*, you have clearly offended some very important people. I think you do not realize what thin ice you are skating on," he said, looking very proud of the expression. "That is the way you say it, yes?"

"More or less." She opened the refrigerator and searched for something to offer him. She had a bottle of inexpensive wine, one can of beer, three diet sodas, and an old head of lettuce. There were teabags and instant coffee in the cupboard. "Would you like some wine?"

He held out his hand. "May I see?"

She gave him the bottle, amused by the look of dismay that spread across his handsome features. "Not up to your standards?"

"It is very pleasant, I am sure," he said carefully. "But perhaps you would make some coffee."

Amanda winced. "Instant."

He started for the door.

"My goodness, I didn't think it was that offensive," she said.

He chuckled. "I am calling for Henri. He will go to the store."

"No," she said so adamantly that he stopped in his tracks and regarded her in astonishment.

"But this is absurd, *ma chérie*. No one can exist like this."

"I exist like this quite nicely. I'm almost never home."

He sighed. "Then we shall drink the wine," he conceded.

"I wouldn't want to insult your palate."

"My palate has survived worse indignities, I assure you." He picked up the bottle. "An opener, *s'il vous plaît.*"

Amanda watched as he went through the entire ritual from sniffing the cork to waving the wine under his nose before tasting it. If his expression was anything to go by, he would not award it top honors. Apparently, however, it ranked well above poison and at least minimally above instant coffee. He poured them each a glass, then lifted his.

"A toast."

Amanda picked up her wine.

"To adventures," he said, his gaze locked with hers.

"To adventures," she echoed weakly and touched her glass to his. She had a feeling that her definition of that word was very different from his. Although she had no doubt that Armand LeConte had been involved in international incidents that would make her blanch, as well as quite a few she would have given anything to be in on, she had a definite hunch that he was referring to amorous pursuits with that toast. She was going to have to engage in some fancy footwork to keep him in line. She decided she'd better get started.

"Who are these important people you feel I've offended?"

"That should be obvious. Your FBI, for starters."

Amanda wanted no part of ownership of Jeffrey Dunne and his cohorts, but she decided to let the possessive pronoun slide for the moment. "Do you have any idea why they would be in such a state over my inquiries?''

"Senator Rawlings spoke with them, did he not?'' he said, settling on the straight-backed kitchen chair as if it were an antique from the court of Louis XIV.

"That was today. The FBI's been bent out of shape for days now." She noticed that he was avoiding her gaze. "You know something, Mr. LeConte. Just tell me and get it over with."

"What have you learned of this Merrill Hudson you were asking about when we spoke?''

"Its overseas headquarters are in Amsterdam. It seems to be the conduit for equipment from a company called Sunland Electronics. The financing is arranged through the National Bank of the Netherlands, courtesy of a woman named Helga Van Sant, who may or may not be exceeding her authority." She watched him closely. "Jump in anytime."

"Why did you go to see Senator Rawlings about this?''

"He's chairman of the Senate Foreign Relations Committee and he and Van Sant are buddies. That suggested to me that he might know about what's going on down here. My hunch is he is either actively involved in the scam, that he is seeing to paperwork personally, or at the very least that he has given the whole thing his tacit approval."

Armand's eyes widened with alarm. "You said this to him?''

"More or less. What's your best guess? Have I hit on the truth?''

"I think you are very lucky he did not have you placed securely behind bars. You do not accuse a United States senator of such things without proof."

"I accused him of nothing. I merely asked the questions."

"I doubt he would comprehend the fine distinction, *ma chérie*. Senator Rawlings is not a sophisticated man."

"You know him, then?"

"But of course. I know many congressmen."

"Yes, you would," she said dully. She had forgotten for just an instant exactly what Armand LeConte did for a living. "Have you had business dealings with him?"

"If you are wondering if he has facilitated my ability to ship guns to foreign countries, the answer is yes. On occasion he has, when it has suited the interests of the United States."

"Whatever that means," Amanda grumbled. "Look, thanks for what you did this afternoon, running down to check on me after Henri put out an alarm." She regarded him closely. "Did you by any chance suggest to your pal the senator that he ought to have the FBI release me?"

His shrug was very Gallic, extremely modest. "We spoke, yes. I do not tell him what to do in matters such as this, however."

"I see. Well, thanks for dropping by. If you think of any information you'd like to share on the record, just give me a call."

Amusement danced in his eyes. "I just did, *ma chérie*," he taunted. He pressed a kiss on each cheek and then vanished through the kitchen door, leaving Amanda to ponder exactly what the hell he thought he'd told her.

\* \* \*

"Dear, Miss Martha's invited us for tea," Amanda's mother announced, hanging up the phone just as Amanda wandered in from the kitchen. "Isn't that lovely?"

"Mother, you go. I think I'll drive back into town and work on this story." She wanted time alone to think through Armand's cryptic remark. "I'll drop you off on my way. I'm sure Miss Martha would be happy to have her driver bring you home."

"Amanda, it is already late afternoon. Your boss has given you the day off. What can you possibly expect to accomplish in the next few hours that you can't do in the morning?" her mother demanded. Her own professional fervor seemed to have lost its glow.

"Probably nothing, but I don't like to lose my focus when I'm in the middle of an investigation. Besides, I need to work. It keeps my mind off of other things."

"No assignment is so important that you can't take a short break to go to tea at a friend's."

Though she didn't begin to understand her mother's insistence, Amanda saw that it would be easier to relent than to argue. She could gulp one cup of tea, eat a couple of petit-fours or a watercress sandwich, and vamoose with a clear conscience.

Miss Martha lived in a lovely brick house with a screened-in porch on the side, a rose garden in the back, several towering oak trees, and enough grounds to qualify the place as an estate. It was about half the size of the senator's. Her mother was suitably impressed anyway, just as Amanda had known she would be. Gracious living was the one thing Elisa Bailey relished. On Long Island she had chosen her friends accordingly.

As they stood on the front stoop, they heard the tap-tap-tap of Miss Martha's cane just before the door swung open. Wearing a pink silk dress with a scarf knotted at the throat, Miss Martha looked ready for a garden party.

"Come in. Come in," she said. "I thought we'd have our tea on the porch. As long as we're having this delightful touch of Indian summer, I want to take advantage of it."

"Indeed, days like this are rare at this time of year in New York," Amanda's mother said, surreptitiously inspecting the decor as Miss Martha led them through the parlor. On the porch, only excellent breeding kept her from flipping over the exquisite, antique porcelain teacups to check for identification.

When Miss Martha was ready to pour the tea, Amanda knew that her mother almost couldn't wait to say, "Oh, please, allow me," just so she could get her hands on the silver teapot. Despite dabbling in journalism over the past few days, it was obvious that her mother's greatest pride was in entertaining and being entertained. Amanda wondered idly how the devil she was going to get her back to it.

Just as she'd been handed her tea, Amanda heard the doorbell and noted the extra cup on the serving tray. That cup made her question the veracity of Miss Martha's exceptionally innocent expression.

"I wonder who that could be," their hostess said, peering intently through the parlor as she waited for her aging housekeeper to answer the door and admit the "unexpected" addition to their little party.

Amanda heard Donelli's voice before she saw him. Her cup rattled in her saucer as she put it back on the table and stood up, glaring at Miss Martha and her mother. She had no doubt that they were in cahoots. They'd probably taken Armand LeConte's impromptu visit this afternoon as a dangerous warning and decided it was time to intercede before Amanda made a rash mistake.

"Well, it's been lovely," she said in a rush. "Too bad I have to get to the office. I'll see you both later." She took a deep breath. "And, by the way, the next time you two want to meddle in a relationship, give Dad a call."

She was almost through the parlor and into the foyer when she bumped straight into Donelli. If the look in his eyes was anything to go by, he was just as stunned as she was. He looked pleased just the same.

"Amanda." His voice was gruffer and less polished than Armand LeConte's but it caressed her name in a convincing way that put the Frenchman's practiced charm to shame.

She couldn't seem to tear her gaze away. "How are you?" The question sounded stiff and formal, especially when she suddenly realized that what she really wanted to ask was whether he missed her half as much as she missed him. The mild flirtation with a sexy, dangerous Frenchman seemed to have whetted her appetite for someone real, someone with a solid physique and a few intriguing scars.

"Okay." His eyes, dark brown and sad, said otherwise. "How about you?"

"Never better. Busy. In fact, I was just on my way out the door. I have to get to the office. I'm on a big story."

A distant feminine chorus again rose in protest, unmuted by Amanda's parting shot. Donelli glanced toward the porch, looking trapped as he realized he was being deserted to what sounded like an all-female garden party. Not willing to get back into the fray, Amanda left him to his fate. She actually made it all the way to her car before he caught up with her.

"Amanda?"

Reluctantly she turned to face him. "Yes."

He looked uncomfortable. "I just wanted you to know that I didn't know anything about this. I know I should have guessed when Miss Martha called, but I didn't. I promised you weeks ago that I would give you time to sort things out and I'm doing my damnedest to live up to my word."

"I believe you. It wouldn't be Miss Martha's style to confide her plans to you," she conceded. "She did it to Mack and me often enough. She and my mother make an indomitable team. Downright scary, in fact."

His eyes widened. "That's who I heard? Your mother's here too?

Amanda couldn't contain a grin. "She didn't warn you about that either?"

"No."

"They're a daunting duo. You could jump in your car and make a break for it. I'd advise it, in fact."

"I'm not a coward, Amanda," he said softly. "Not like you."

She regarded him with sudden fury, a compilation of all the past days' irritations, only some of which were his responsibility. "Dammit, Joe Donelli, I am not a coward. Of all people, you should know that."

He shook his head. "A brave woman would stick around and see this through, Amanda. After all, it's just a cup of tea and a little friendly conversation."

"That's what you think," she muttered. Those two would have them walking down the aisle by suppertime.

Donelli ignored the sarcastic remark. He appeared to be on a roll.

"A brave woman would sit down and talk to me and try to work things out. A brave woman would not slam the door on a relationship that had everything going for it. A brave woman, dammit, would take a risk."

She scowled at him. "I did that once. I got burned."

"And my best friend got killed because of something I did," he shot back angrily. "Are you telling me that shouldn't have mattered to me? That I always have to choose you over my conscience?"

When he put it that way, he made her seem . . . petty. She regarded him miserably. "I don't know, Joe. I really don't know anymore. I just can't forget about trust," she said quietly and climbed into her car. She rolled down her window. "If you can think of any way to get that back, let me know."

She waited for a minute, but the request had left him speechless, just as she had known it would. As she drove off, she watched in the rearview mirror as he stood staring after her, his hands shoved in his pockets.

She muttered a curse. Maybe Miss Martha had had the right idea trying to force the issue. The last few minutes had reminded her that all of the powerful emotions were still in place—the hurt, the anger, the pride, the love. These months apart hadn't solved anything. The problem was that she was scared, terrified, in fact, of acting on those feelings.

It all kept coming back to trust. Unfortunately, trust didn't just materialize out of the blue. It came one slow, careful day at a time. And once lost, the road to reclaiming it was longer than ever.

One day, one step at a time, Amanda sighed. It was up to her whether she dared to take the first one.

# CHAPTER

## *Seventeen*

It was dark by the time Amanda reached the outskirts of downtown Atlanta. Maybe she'd grown overly confident with Armand's watchdog always right behind her, but she didn't notice the black limousine until it was almost too late. It followed her into the parking garage at a clip that would have made Jim Harrison's radar guns go into spasms of ecstasy.

When she tried to swerve out of its way, it followed, blocking her path of retreat and forcing her into an angled space. The men who emerged didn't look like your average Hollywood celebrities or the talent coordinators for *Star Search*. She had a feeling they would have fit right in with a lineup of menacing, stereotypical Middle Eastern terrorists.

As she considered the last time she'd seen a limo like this one, she touched the still-healing scar on her cheek.

A smidgen of anxiety crept through her. Since there was no immediate route of escape, she decided it would be best if they didn't see even a hint of her fear.

"Excuse me, but around here we like to park in the spaces, not across them," she explained cheerfully as she tried to take mental notes on their distinguishing features on the off chance that she survived to describe them. One was young, about twenty-five or so, and exceedingly plump, the other older and painfully thin. The Abbott and Costello of terrorists, she thought, though no one seemed to be laughing. Startlingly blue eyes, set deep in swarthy complexions, regarded her intently.

"We believe it would be a mistake for you to write this story, young miss," said the older, thin one.

As long as one of them didn't pull out an AK-47 and aim it at her, she was willing to consider all points of view. "Oh? And why is that?"

"We do not believe you would portray our people in a positive light."

Arab PR people? Amanda thought in amazement. They had an interesting technique. "Perhaps you would like to come inside and give me your thoughts on this on the record. Do you represent your government?"

"No, young miss," the older one said adamantly. "We are simple businessmen."

*Isn't everyone these days*, Amanda thought dryly. "From?"

"We were born in Iraq. We are Americans now."

"Why do you object to the story I'm working on? How do you even know about it?" Hell, at the rate word was getting around, it would be on the front cover of some biannual report before she could gather all her facts.

"We know, that is all. You are very intelligent. I am sure you understand what we are saying. It would be very bad for you to do this story."

"Very bad," the heavier man echoed, suddenly finding his voice after keeping silent up until now. Maybe he was supposed to represent the muscle of this duo. If so, he'd gone a little too obviously to flab.

"We are prepared to make it worth your while to forget all about it," the first man said, reaching into the backseat of the limousine and pulling out a briefcase. Gucci. As bribes went, it wasn't bad.

"Sorry. I already have a briefcase," Amanda said, just as he popped the latch and displayed what seemed to be a very large amount of cash, far more than her checking account had ever seen at one time.

"Holy shit," she muttered under her breath. She recalled the old days when a bottle of liquor from a source was considered ethically suspect. "Thanks for thinking of me, but I don't think so." The words didn't exactly trip off her tongue, but she was proud of herself for getting them out at all.

The round-faced man, still young enough to be impressed by riches no doubt, regarded her in astonishment. "It is a lot of money," he said indignantly.

"I can see that, but that's not the way it works. I report the news. I don't take bribes to cover it up."

"Bribe is such an ugly word," the older man said sorrowfully. "This is a gift, an expression of our gratitude."

"Exactly why would anyone be this grateful? I must be on to a helluva story."

"It is important only to us, I assure you," he said.

"You, the FBI, an arms dealer, an electronics expert, a banker, and at least one senator I can name. Kinda makes me wonder how it all fits together. Leave me your card and I'll get back to you.''

''No, young miss. If you do not do as we ask, I assure you that we will get back to you.'' Although it was subtle, there was no mistaking the menace underlying the statement.

He snapped the briefcase closed and held it out. Amanda put her hands behind her back and clenched them tightly together. They seemed to be itching to clutch that briefcase. He shrugged.

''You understand we mean you no harm,'' he said with great sincerity. It didn't ring true after the implied threat only seconds before.

''But we must look out for the best interests of our people,'' the other said.

Amanda nodded sympathetically. ''We all do what we have to do.''

They bowed. Apparently her sarcasm had slipped past them. It was probably just as well. She didn't want to imagine what the next briefcase they dropped off was likely to contain.

She didn't wait around to watch them depart, though she did sneak a peak at the limo's tag number. Probably a rental, but it was worth checking out. In the elevator, out of sight of their disconcerting gazes, she jotted down that tag number. Then her knees turned to jelly.

What on earth had she stumbled into? Arab-American businessmen wanted to pay her off. The FBI and a U.S. senator were ready to lock her up. And an international arms dealer was offering her tips so subtle that she couldn't begin to figure them out.

The only light on in the *Inside Atlanta* newsroom was in Oscar's office. Still shaky from an encounter that could have turned ugly, Amanda walked in and sank down on a chair across from him. She reached for the bottle of scotch he hadn't had time to hide, glanced around for a second glass, didn't see one, and drank straight from the bottle. The liquor burned all the way down. She shuddered.

Oscar went absolutely still as he observed her uncharacteristic behavior. "You hate scotch," he said finally, as if she'd needed reminding.

"Desperate women do desperate things," she said and took one more swallow of the hateful stuff. Her jittery nerves finally began to settle down.

Oscar came out from behind the desk and snatched the bottle from her, probably because it was nearing empty and he couldn't bear to part with the final shots. "Want to tell me what this is all about?"

"I was just confronted in our parking garage by two men who don't like my current investigation."

His eyes widened. "You okay? They didn't hurt you, did they? I'll call Harrison." He was already reaching for the phone.

"Don't bother. They didn't hurt me. They offered me a briefcase full of money to back off." She held out her empty hands to reassure him. "I didn't take it."

Oscar looked hurt. "I never thought you would. How much money?"

"I'd say a few hundred thousand by the look of it. I didn't count it."

"Holy shit!"

"My reaction exactly. Why would two Arab-Americans be so damned determined to stop me from pursuing this story? Is any of this adding up for you yet?"

Oscar shook his head. "Let's line up who we have here," he suggested.

He sat down and poured himself the last of the scotch. It filled a glass. Amanda regarded it longingly.

"I've done that," she said. "On one side, we have some opportunists, maybe a few misguided idealists who figure the Iraqis have every bit as much right to high tech weaponry as the rest of us. On the other side, we have the U.S. government, which is supposed to be blocking such sales, but, in this instance, anyway, doesn't seem to be."

"It wouldn't be the first time that public policy and covert activities haven't exactly matched up," he reminded her. "That's the story, Amanda."

It made sense, she thought as she went to her desk, but she just couldn't seem to muster up any enthusiasm for that scenario. Something about it didn't ring true, but damned if she could think of why.

It all came back to the government and whether it was turning a blind eye to the shipments of technology, and if so, at what level.

That was a question Calvin Jones or Graham Hudson could answer. If one of them didn't spill the beans, she might fly back to Virginia and torment Armand LeConte until he gave her an explanation that wasn't another riddle.

And if any one of them professed to be a simple businessman one more time, she was going to threaten to infect their computer systems with the deadliest virus she could figure out how to program in. She sighed. Without Richard Howell's computer expertise, it wasn't much of a threat, but maybe they wouldn't realize that.

She checked the phone book for Jones's address. It was no surprise to discover that he wasn't listed. She went over to Jack Davis's Rolodex and flipped through the cards. Sure enough, like any self-respecting journal-

ist, he'd wrangled that home phone and address, probably when he did that feature for the *Constitution* a few
years back.

While she was at it, she found a corporate directory
and tracked down the business number for Merrill
Hudson in Amsterdam. If she couldn't get Jones to talk,
she could call Graham Hudson at work. It would be
morning in Europe in just a couple of hours.

"I'm out of here," she called to Oscar on her way to
the elevator.

He came to the door of his office and regarded her
anxiously. "You want company?"

She shook her head. "I'll be fine. I'm going to track
down Calvin Jones and have another chat with him."

"You call me when you leave there," he said. "I'll
stick around here until I hear from you."

"It's not necessary."

"Just for once, will you do what I tell you?"

"I'll call. Stop worrying. Henri is usually hot on my
trail."

"Who the devil's Henri?"

"LeConte's personally assigned bodyguard."

"Where was he when you were being accosted in the
parking garage?" Oscar inquired.

Amanda didn't have an answer for that one, and, to
be perfectly honest, she didn't like the implications.
Once before in her career, she had counted on the
presence of an unwanted but dutiful bodyguard only to
discover later that he'd been conked on the head and
taken out of commission.

"I'll be careful," she said firmly.

Oscar gave her a wry look. "Why doesn't that
reassure me?"

"Just give it a rest," she grumbled as the elevator doors slid shut.

Calvin Jones wasn't home. In fact, as she waited down the block for nearly an hour, she began to get the oddest sensation that she was wasting her time. Maybe it was the drawn drapes, the lack of any welcoming light burning inside or out. The man had small children who should have been in bed by now, tucked in by his wife or a babysitter. Maybe it was just gut instinct that made her believe he'd taken off for parts unknown, dragging the whole family with him. Maybe Buffalo. Maybe Amsterdam. Maybe on a vacation in the Caymans for all she knew. Wherever he'd gone, it appeared he wasn't about to provide her with any information. Not tonight anyway.

She could wait until tomorrow and try to catch him at the office or she could skip a step and call Graham Hudson. She checked her watch. If he was as compulsive as most businessmen, he might be in by now.

She pulled into an all-night store, bought a diet soda, then went to the pay phone, hoping for a better connection than she'd get on her car phone. She punched in the overseas number, then followed that with her phone car access number and listened to the distant ringing. No answer. Apparently it was still too early. She'd have to call again from home.

She hung up and glanced around the parking lot. Henri, it seemed, was back on the job. So, unfortunately, was Jeffrey Dunne. She walked over to him.

"Okay, what's the deal?"

"Just keeping an eye on you."

"For whom?"

"Does it matter?"

"It might clarify a few things."

"Sorry. I'm just along to see that you don't pester the good senator with any more wild accusations."

"On whose orders?" she demanded.

"I got my instructions the usual way, from my boss. No telling where he got his."

Amanda gave up that line of questioning. If he had nothing better to do than trail her around, it was just more proof of how the government wasted the taxpayers' dollars. She dug in her purse and pulled out the tag number she'd taken from the limo earlier. "Just so this jaunt won't be wasted for both of us, then, how about checking this out for me?" She handed him the slip of paper.

"What's this?"

"The tag number from a limo."

"You're going about this dating business all wrong, Amanda."

"Very funny. Can you check it out for me?"

"Of course I can. Why would I want to?"

"Because the men in that car tried to give me a whole lot of money to forget this investigation."

His expression grim, he waved her into the car and picked up his cellular phone. He identified himself to whomever he had called, then read off the number, his troubled gaze all the while locked on Amanda. That's how she knew that whatever information he was given was about as innocuous as gunfire from an Uzi.

He slowly hung up the phone, looking even more exasperated than usual.

"Okay, Amanda," he said wearily, "what the hell have you gotten yourself into?"

# CHAPTER

## Eighteen

"WHAT do you mean by that?" Amanda demanded, scowling at the FBI agent. "You know perfectly well what I've been investigating. Why are you suddenly so jumpy? Who does that car belong to?"

"I can't say," Dunne said, now suddenly avoiding her gaze.

"What do you mean you can't say?"

"I mean the information is classified."

"Since when is a car registration classified?"

"Since now."

Amanda lost patience. "Now this minute? Now because I'm the one who's asking?"

"Now because that's the way it is."

"Goddammit, don't you know any language but government doublespeak?"

"Sorry. My lines are scripted here."

"Well, so are mine," she said coldly. "I'm out of here."

"Amanda, wait."

"For what? More of your infamous runaround. I don't think so."

"Amanda!" He grabbed her wrist to prevent her from getting out of the car.

She glared at him. "You planning to kidnap me like you did last time?"

His grip eased. "Sorry. I guess you're right. There's nothing more to say."

She marched across the parking lot, got into her car, and drove away. She noted that only one car followed. It wasn't Jeffrey Dunne. It was probably just as well. She might have been tempted to try to run him off the road.

If Dunne wouldn't tell her who that limo belonged to, then she'd go to Jim Harrison. The mere fact that the FBI agent was so tight-lipped would intrigue the detective. As she headed for home, she punched in his number on her car phone. Despite the hour, he was still at work.

"What's up?" he wanted to know at once. "You promised to call right after you got through searching Howell's house. That was yesterday. It makes me very nervous when I don't hear the sound of you rattling cages for that long."

"I know and I'm sorry. It's been a very strange couple of days. If you've got a couple of minutes, I'll fill you in."

"You want to stop by here?"

"No. I'm beat. We'll do this while I head for home, if you don't mind."

"Go for it."

She ran through her discovery of the letter in Howell's

computer files, her meeting with Senator Rawlings, being taken in by the FBI, and that little scene in the parking garage earlier.

"Now I want to know who those two guys were. Can you check it out? Here's the tag number." For a moment, she decided against telling him that Jeffrey Dunne had already run the same check.

"Give me a minute," he said. "I'll put you on hold and see what I get."

Amanda turned on the car radio and realized it was still set on Donelli's favorite country station. It had been set there the last time she'd tuned in and hearing his favorite songs had made her so melancholy she'd switched it off at once without changing the dial. Now she listened as all those mournful melodies echoed her own thoughts. No wonder people got caught up in country music. It captured some of life's elemental truths, especially when it came to love.

She was sinking deeper and deeper into a glorious funk when Harrison came back on the line.

"This is the damnedest thing I ever came across," he said, sounding more mystified than annoyed.

"Why?"

"DMV won't say a thing. In fact, the contact I have over there couldn't get me off the line fast enough."

"What do you make of that?"

"I'd say that car has diplomatic status. Or it's part of some very hush-hush undercover operation."

"By the FBI," Amanda said automatically.

"Uh-uh, Amanda. If I'm right, you've skipped right on over to the big time. I'd say this covert game belongs to the CIA."

Amanda hit the brakes so hard that she was surprised

the car didn't end up standing straight up on its front bumper. "You're kidding me, right?"

"I don't know anything for a fact, but I'm not kidding," he assured her.

"The CIA does not operate inside the U.S.," she reminded him.

"Not supposed to," he agreed, leaving her to draw her own conclusions.

Amanda started thinking about all the things that hadn't quite fit. This could explain them. "But you think if it involves a covert operation outside the U.S.," she improvised, "they might just poke their noses around inside our borders if someone happens to endanger their scheme."

"Makes perfect sense to me."

"Of course, those tags could have been diplomatic," Amanda said, trying to tame her wild imagination. "Just because those men said they didn't represent their government doesn't mean they were telling the truth. They could have been a pair of Iraqi embassy workers."

"I don't think there are a lot of those around these days. We shipped the lot of them home, remember?"

"How about at the United Nations? They've got people there."

"And you think they skipped out of New York just to pay a call on you?"

"They had hundreds of thousands of dollars in that briefcase. I don't think they were going to squabble over gas mileage."

"Do you want them to be diplomats or do you want them to be CIA?"

"I want them to leave me alone," she said plaintively.

He chuckled. "Then I suggest you wrap up this story and get them off your back once and for all."

"Easier said than done, Harrison."

Of course, she thought as she hung up, if the detective was right about the CIA, then it was possible she was much closer to a solution than she realized.

By the time Amanda turned into her driveway twenty minutes later, her brain was functioning at warp speed, but her body felt as if it had been hit by a truck. The last of her adrenaline had apparently been used up on the outskirts of town. She could hardly wait to take a warm shower and collapse into bed.

Unfortunately, judging from the number of lights on all over the house and the number of cars in the driveway, that wasn't going to happen anytime soon.

She recognized one car as Miss Martha's sporty little compact, the one she'd given up driving several years earlier. Amanda had a hunch Miss Martha had loaned it to her mother, rather than sending her home with her driver. The second car was a mystery. She wasn't at all sure she was up for discovering the solution tonight.

She went inside anyway and found her mother sitting stiffly in a chair, her expression every bit as stubborn as Amanda's on one of her most belligerent days. Across from her sat Nelson Bailey. His eyes lit up when he saw her.

"Pumpkin!" he said. He took a few steps toward her, then faltered when he recognized that she wasn't welcoming him with open arms.

"Dad," she said cautiously, watching her mother for some clue about the state of affairs between her parents. It didn't look as if a truce had been declared, but obviously there was no open warfare at the moment. She glanced back at her father. "I'll leave you two to talk."

"No!" both parents protested at once.

Amanda came very close to moaning aloud. "I really am not up to mediating your problems at the moment."

His eyes on Amanda, her father said, "I came down here to apologize. Your mother refuses to listen."

"Apologize?" her mother retorted. "You call that an apology?"

"I told you I wanted you back home."

"For what? To make sure the laundry gets done?"

Amanda thought they were doing just fine without her, but she hesitated to move and disturb the exchange.

"I can do my own damn laundry," her father grumbled.

"Then why the hell do you need me?"

"Because I love you, dammit."

His uncensored response hung in the air for several seconds before Elisa Bailey blinked away a tear and said softly, "You do?"

"Well, of course I do," Amanda's father said impatiently. "That was never the issue."

"Then would you mind telling me what was?" Amanda demanded, indignant on her mother's behalf.

She turned and glared at her mother. She could see that those three little words, *I love you*, had sapped the fight right out of her. "And what about a career?" she asked her. "It was important enough that you butted into mine. Have you told him how you felt about that?"

"Stay out of this, Amanda," they both said, not taking their eyes off of each other. Enough electricity was being generated by that look to light up rural Georgia, if not downtown Atlanta.

Amanda looked from one to the other and shook her head. She might as well go and make reservations for them on the first flight to New York in the morning.

And then she probably ought to get the hell out and give them some privacy.

# CHAPTER

## *Nineteen*

OUTSIDE, with the air turning chill, Amanda sat in her car trying to figure out where she could go so that her parents could be alone. It wasn't as if there was a hotel on every block out here. There weren't even blocks, just miles and miles of peach orchards and farmland and a few scattered clusters of buildings that folks in these parts considered towns. She couldn't imagine driving all the way back into Atlanta or even over to Athens. Nor were there many places nearby where the welcome mat would be out. Not that people weren't neighborly. They just weren't nearby.

Which brought her back to Joe. He was only a few miles away. He would welcome her. Maybe.

Each time Amanda recalled the way the hurt and anguish on her mother's face had disappeared when her repentant father had declared that his love for her had never been at issue, she couldn't help thinking about her own situation. No matter how hard she had tried to block out her feelings for Donelli, no matter how much self-righteous fury she had indulged in, the bottom line had never changed. She still loved him. Her life was emptier without him.

Forging a new relationship, however, was not going to be easy. Some things would have to change . . . for both of them. And the only way that could begin to happen was to start talking. He had left the ball solidly in her court. It was time she picked it up and ran with it or found some way to finally let go. Since the latter seemed impossible, she was left to act on the former.

Drawing in a deep breath and firming up her resolve, she started the car and turned onto the highway leading away from her house and toward his. Despite the hour, she knew he would still be up. Except during planting season, he was a night owl.

As she pulled to a stop in front of the house, she noted that the porch light was still on, as was a low light in his bedroom. Although she still had her own key, a rare uncertainty swept through her. She rang the doorbell and waited. As she listened for the sound of his footsteps, she kept glancing toward her car as if judging how long it might take her to reach it and flee. Then, before she could come to a decision about whether to go or stay, he was there.

For the space of a heartbeat, neither of them said a word. Amanda couldn't seem to take her eyes off of his tousled dark brown hair and bare chest and the jeans that rode low on his hips. He looked leaner, more desirable than ever. And the expression of smoldering appreciation in his eyes echoed her reaction.

"Well," he said finally. "This is a surprise."

On some level it seemed to register that he wasn't stepping aside, but she was too busy spilling nervous words on top of each other to take much notice.

"I'm in the middle of this investigation and it's gotten pretty complicated with the FBI and now the CIA and who knows who else. Anyway, I've been thinking of you. Especially because of the mess between my mother and my father. Did you know about that? Anyway, I think it's resolved. I'm pretty sure she's going back to New York with my father in the morning. Thank God, that crisis has been averted and they're together again. Anyway, I really could use your input on this investigation. I can't seem to sort it all out and you're so logical, I thought maybe you could help. If you have the time, that is."

A smile came and went before sober eyes regarded her intently. "I'd be happy to help, Amanda. You know that."

"Terrific." She started to step inside, then realized that he hadn't budged. She looked into his eyes and saw... regret? Or worse, pity?

"But not tonight," he said.

"Not tonight?" she repeated, her throat suddenly dry. She would not ask why. She would not indulge in guesswork. She would not slam him in the jaw, which was what she very much wanted to do at this moment.

"Virginia's in the morning?" he suggested. "I can be there by eight."

Her chin rose a notch. "I don't want to put you to too much trouble."

"You know it's no trouble, Amanda," he said in a tone that chided her for her sarcasm. "Eight, okay?"

"Sure, whatever," she said with what she hoped like hell was an indifferent shrug.

"See you," he said in that soft, sexy voice that wrapped itself around her like a cloak.

Determinedly fighting the impact of that low, provocative tone, she turned on her heel and left without another word. She was at the end of the lane, ready to turn onto the highway, before she allowed one single, humiliating tear to fall.

Calling herself everything from a fool to a masochist, she vowed to let Donelli sit in Virginia's scoffing up pancakes from now until doomsday . . . alone. She would wrap up this investigation on her own, just as she always had . . . alone. She didn't need Donelli's help.

She didn't need Donelli. *She did not need Donelli*. If she said that often enough, it would have to be true. Wouldn't it?

Amanda still didn't have the answer to that question by the time she drove straight past Virginia's at sixty miles per hour the next morning precisely at eight o'clock. Donelli was just parking his car. There wasn't a chance in hell that he missed her cruising by, thumbing her nose at him.

He overtook her on the freeway, drove alongside to make sure she was aware of his presence, then pulled into the lane directly behind her. Judging from the expression on his face, he wasn't pleased. Terrific. Neither was she.

She had had a long, lonely night . . . in her car, in her own damn driveway . . . to ponder exactly what kind of game he'd been playing the night before. The choices ranged from a mere display of power to the presence of another woman. She wasn't wild about either of these alternatives or, for that matter, any of the lesser possibilities in between.

In the downtown highrise that housed the *Inside Atlanta* offices, Amanda snagged the last remaining parking place on level three and prayed like crazy that it would take Donelli another ten minutes to find a parking place. That might give her just enough time to figure out what she was going to say to him when he came storming into the newsroom.

"Morning, Amanda," the temporary receptionist chirped cheerfully as Amanda exited the elevator. "I have some messages for you. Should I go through them?"

"Not now. I have to get inside."

The friendly woman immediately looked worried. "Is everything okay?"

"Let's just say bombs over Beirut probably don't make any more noise than the explosion you're likely to hear in the newsroom in about five minutes."

Oscar obviously overheard the exchange and stepped out of his office. "Okay, Amanda, what have you gone and done now?"

"Nothing," she said, then injected a note of fierce determination into her voice. "Yet." When he started to say more, she told him firmly, "This doesn't have anything to do with you. No matter what happens in the next few minutes, I want you to remember that."

Just then the stairwell door burst open and Donelli stormed through. He wasn't even breathing hard. Oscar's eyes lit up.

"Not a word," Amanda warned him.

Donelli latched on to Amanda's arm with a grip that could have won arm-wrestling matches in one of those country bars frequented by pro-circuit wannabes. "We need someplace private," he said to Oscar. "What's available?"

Amanda's glare kept Oscar silent.

"The conference room," the receptionist suggested, eyes wide.

"We do not need privacy," Amanda bit out, her teeth clenched and her heels dug into the carpet.

There was an unyielding glint in Donelli's eyes that warned her he'd lost his patience somewhere in Gwinnett County. She matched him glare for glare. His voice dropped to a quiet, deadly serious tone. "There's an alternative to you walking into that conference room on your own. You won't like it."

A liberated woman would have told him exactly what he could do with his threats. Amanda almost told him. Then she considered the fact that the end result would essentially be the same. She would wind up in that conference room and she would probably have suffered the indignity of having been tossed over his shoulder for the trip. Not a soul in this place would jump to her assistance. The receptionist was getting too big a kick out of this whole episode. Oscar thought Donelli walked on water. Jack Davis probably hadn't engaged in physical activity since high school gym class. Larry was out somewhere shooting pictures of birds or something.

Amanda drew herself up, stiffened her back, and stalked into the conference room. Although she absolutely refused to glance back, she thought she caught the traitorous Oscar giving Donelli an encouraging thumbs up. She knew she heard the faint hint of a low chuckle. The man was getting a real charge out of this. It probably appealed to that mile-wide macho streak that he and Donelli shared.

In the conference room, she resolved to snatch the initiative right out of Joe's hands. She whirled and said, "So, what do you know about the computer software needed for SCUD missiles?"

He gave her a wry look as he slowly closed the door. He took a determined step toward her.

"What about the parts for a B-57 bomber?" she persisted, backing up.

His gaze pinned on her, he just stepped closer. The silent approach was definitely unnerving. She ran through a long list of questions before she found herself flat against the far wall of the conference room. Donelli was still advancing, an amused smile playing about his lips.

When there was nowhere left for her to run, he stood toe-to-toe, his hands braced against the wall on either side of her. "Finished?" he inquired in that lazy drawl that still hadn't lost its Brooklyn accent.

Amanda swallowed hard. "Not exactly."

"Then be quick about it, because I have waited a very long time for this kiss and I'm getting impatient."

A faint spirit of rebellion tried to get a toehold amid the excitement that was suddenly rampaging through Amanda. "If you think you're going to kiss me after the way you jerked me around last night, you're crazy," she said.

Apparently there wasn't much conviction in her tone, because he laughed. He laughed just long enough to thoroughly infuriate her all over again, and then, just when she opened her mouth to protest, he kissed her.

The kiss was long and slow and deep. And when it was over, a breathtaking eternity later, he followed up with a succession of quick, soft kisses that teased. And then capped it off with one more intended to melt her bones, her resolve, and anything else that couldn't withstand that degree of heat.

"Oh, shit," she murmured when he was through. To her everlasting regret, she sounded a little drunk.

Donelli grinned. No, actually, he smirked.

"Now that that's out of the way, why don't you explain what that little act of yours was all about this morning?" he suggested. He sat down at the conference table, tilted his chair back, and regarded her intently as he waited for her reply. A psychiatrist awaiting a breakthrough response from a patient couldn't have looked any more expectant.

Amanda couldn't seem to recall her name, much less anything that had happened prior to the last five minutes. Then the memories began to penetrate the fog that had steamed up her senses.

"You had a woman in the house with you last night, didn't you?"

"Is that a concern of yours?" he asked evenly. "You told me weeks ago you never wanted to see me again."

That slowed her down, but she wasn't interested in accuracy at the moment. "Was there or wasn't there a woman there last night?"

"There was."

She swallowed hard. She'd been hoping against hope that she'd been wrong. Before she could think of another thing to say, he added, "Is that a problem?"

"You're damn right it's a problem," she snapped before she could stop herself.

"Why?"

"Because you're supposed to be in love with me, not chasing other women."

"I repeat, you told me in no uncertain terms that you never wanted to see me again."

Amanda paced from one end of the conference room to the other as she contemplated the best way to respond to that. "I lied," she said finally. She planted her feet apart and her hands on her hips and glared down at him. "I lied, dammit, and you should have known that."

A slow, satisfied smile spread across his face. "You lied, huh?"

"Okay, I said it. You don't have to rub it in."

He reached out, snagged her wrist and tried to tumble her into his lap. She didn't go quite as easily as he'd obviously thought she would, but she didn't put up much of a struggle.

"That doesn't mean everything is okay with us," she warned. "We still have a lot to work out."

"I know."

"I still don't like what you did to me with the FBI."

"I know."

"From now on there are no secrets between us."

"Okay."

He was being so agreeable, she thought she'd risk one more question. "So, who was she?"

"Who was who?"

"The woman who was there last night."

"My ex-wife."

Amanda's mouth dropped open. "What the hell was she doing there?"

"She dropped in to say hi."

"All the way from New York? Just to say hi?"

"So she said."

"She wants you back."

"I don't think so."

"Joe, of course she does. Why else would she come all this way?"

He grinned. "Jealous, aren't you?"

"Of your ex-wife? Absolutely not."

"Then why all the questions?"

"Because you're too damned trusting for your own good. Somebody has to warn you about the wiles of that devious woman. She walked out on you when you needed her the most. Have you forgotten that?"

"If you want to warn somebody about her wiles, I suggest you stop by the house and tell her new husband."

"New husband?" she repeated weakly before relief began flooding through her. Then, because he'd tricked her into putting all of her vulnerabilities on the line, she punched him in the chest. "You said you were in that house with a woman last night."

"I was."

"You knew what I meant and you deliberately let me think that you were in there fooling around."

"When you're a drowning man, you grab whatever lifeline is in the vicinity."

"Is that your way of saying you've missed me?"

"You know I have."

"Good. Then you can help me nail down the last few pieces of this investigation. You're gonna love it. The FBI is involved, maybe even the CIA."

His gaze narrowed. "Are you deliberately trying to provoke me?"

"Nope. I just want to test where your loyalties will fall this time." She'd meant the remark to tease, but there was an underlying note of seriousness that neither of them could mistake.

"Amanda," he warned. "No games. No tests. Either you still love me or you don't."

"I still love you," she admitted. "That doesn't mean I'm ready to trust you yet. That could take a little longer. I've mentioned that before. It hasn't gone away."

He stood up and deposited her on her feet in front of him. Suddenly he looked very tired. "I have no intention of jumping through hoops to prove anything to you," he said flatly. "If you don't know how I feel about you by now, then we have nothing more to talk about."

The thought of letting go again was almost more than she could bear, but she couldn't commit to any more than trying again. "Help me with this investigation, please. Then we'll see."

"What exactly do you want me to do?"

"I want you to talk to Jeffrey Dunne."

"You know him. You talk to him."

"He won't tell me anything."

He shrugged. "Then there's nothing I can do. If he won't tell you, he won't tell me."

"You're so damned tight with the FBI, of course he will," she snapped without thinking. The look of condemnation that spread across Donelli's face cut straight through her.

"And if I pass this test, Amanda, if I get him to talk to me and then I turn the information over to you, will you be satisfied? Will I have earned your trust again?" He shook his head. "Forget it, sweetheart. I don't like the rules. And, frankly, I'm not so sure I like what they tell me about how far you'll go to get a story."

He turned and walked out, slamming the conference room door behind him so hard that the walls shook. He left Amanda to wonder exactly which one of them had really flunked this test she'd dreamed up.

"Amanda? Amanda, honey, are you okay?" Jenny Lee asked hours later.

Amanda looked up from the row of jelly beans she'd line up across her desk. "What?"

"Are you okay?"

"Just dandy," she replied.

"Oscar told me Joe was here."

"Yes."

"Did you all have another fight?"

"You could say that."

Jenny Lee put an arm around her shoulders and squeezed. "You'll work it out. I just know you will."

Amanda regarded her bleakly. "I don't think so. I think I really blew it this time."

"Well, I think I have something here that will cheer you up."

When Amanda didn't react, Jenny Lee carefully extracted an envelope from her purse and placed it in front of her. "Read it," she insisted.

"Later."

"No, Amanda. Now!"

The sharp tone with its faint hint of excitement finally got Amanda's attention. There was a single page in the envelope, a letter addressed to Helga Van Sant.

*Dear Ms. Van Sant:*

*This is to officially inform you that you are to approve any loans necessary to the Sunland Electronics Corporation pursuant to their agreement with Merrill Hudson. This is a matter of utmost important and you have my personal assurance that your actions in this matter will be carefully protected and held confidential by the full authority of my office.*

*Yours very truly,*
*Senator Blaine Rawlings*

\* \* \*

Amanda couldn't contain a whoop of excitement. "Do you realize what this means?"

"Why, of course I do," Jenny Lee replied. "It's the evidence you need to pull this story together."

"Or at least to make a few key people squirm until they talk. How'd you get it?"

"One of the girls at the bank today. She was Richard's girlfriend. She mentioned she had something he'd given her for safekeeping and she didn't know what to do with it. I asked her if I could see it. She gave me the letter."

"Well, hallelujah and amen!" Amanda said. "I think my favorite good ol' boy has a lot of explaining to do."

# CHAPTER

## Twenty

LETTER in hand, Amanda drove to Senator Blaine Rawlings's office, trailed by what she'd come to accept as her usual coterie of watchdogs. As soon as Jeffrey Dunne realized exactly where she was headed, he bounded across the parking garage after her. She deliberately allowed the elevator door to close in his face. His muttered curse followed her as the elevator climbed.

She walked into the senator's penthouse suite of offices and was pleased to note that several people seemed to recognize her. They'd probably had a Wanted poster made up just for her. None of them seemed pleased to see her, although quite a few sprang to their feet and headed in her direction.

"Don't mind me," she said. "I just want to have a word with the senator."

Gregory Fine, the senator's longtime assistant and a man who did love the power that gave him, stepped into her path. "I really don't think the senator has time to see you this morning. His schedule is jam-packed."

"Then unjam it," she suggested.

His patently false smile vanished. "Just who do you think you're talking to?"

"'Whom,'" she corrected pleasantly.

She handed him a copy of the letter. She'd put the original in the *Inside Atlanta* safe and brought three copies along just in case someone decided to do what Gregory Fine was likely to do in the next thirty seconds.

Sure enough, he took one look at the implicating page, turned pale, and zipped it into the office shredder so quickly that Amanda was surprised he hadn't gotten his hideous brown and orange tie caught in the machine as well.

When he was sure the damaging evidence was mutilated, he turned back to her and demanded, "Where the hell did you get that?"

"Sorry. I can't say," Amanda said, enjoying turning the tables on officialdom for a change. "Offhand, though, I'd say that letter contains the secret password that gets me in to see the senator."

His expression turned ugly. "What letter?"

"The original of the one you just shredded."

For an instant he looked disconcerted. "You have the original?"

"You betcha," she said. "Now, do I get in or do I go to print with what I have? I'd just love to quote the senator as saying *no comment* on this."

Gregory Fine knew exactly what inference would be made if the senator declined to comment. As much as he hated giving in to her, he trudged off toward the senator's private domain. A moment later he beckoned to Amanda.

"The senator will see you now," he said stiffly.

"How lovely."

She walked in, noting that Senator Rawlings seemed to have forgotten his manners again. He didn't rise to greet her. He didn't smile. Hell, he didn't even nod to acknowledge her presence. In fact, he was on the phone.

"Joel Crenshaw, please," he said with a pointed look at her.

Terrific, Amanda thought. He was calling her publisher. Fortunately, Joel didn't like being intimidated any better than she did.

"I have one of your reporters here," the senator said in his most jovial good ol' boy tone. "Yes. That's her name. The same one I had picked up by the FBI the other day. I thought that had settled the matter, but she hasn't seemed to get the message. Perhaps you should join us over here."

Amanda couldn't hear Joel's response, but the senator seemed satisfied.

"Let's talk about this letter," Amanda said when he'd hung up.

"There is no letter," he said.

Amanda handed over a copy to jog his obviously faulty short-term memory. "Looks like a letter to me. Your official stationery, your signature."

"Ms. Roberts, I do not intend to discuss this letter with you now or at any time in the future."

She shrugged. "Okay by me. I can go with a *no comment* response."

"There will be no story," he said flatly.

She regarded him incredulously. "I beg your pardon."

"Are you deaf too, girl? I said there would be no story. As soon as that boss of yours gets here, we'll talk this out and that'll be the end of it."

"I don't think so," she said, but she was beginning to get a very odd feeling in the pit of her stomach. Senator Rawlings seemed awfully sure of himself, downright confident, in fact.

Since he didn't seem inclined to elaborate on his plans before Joel's arrival, they sat there staring at each other, taking each other's measure. The senator looked tired and definitely irritable. To her bemusement, he didn't appear trapped.

The buzz of his phone shattered the stalemate. He answered. "Yes. Send him in."

Amanda turned toward the door, expecting to see Joel. Instead, Jeffrey Dunne stood there.

"Come on in," the senator said jovially. "We're waiting for a few more people."

Amanda exchanged a look with the FBI agent that told her he was no more certain what he was doing here than she was anymore.

The next time the door to the office opened the man who walked through was one of the two who'd offered her a hefty bribe for her silence. He nodded politely, then moved to a far corner of the room, as if seeking shadows. The behavior of a CIA operative, Amanda suddenly decided.

Five minutes later the door burst open and Joel and Oscar stormed in without waiting to be announced.

"I don't appreciate your holding one of my reporters this way, Senator," Joel said, taking a place behind Amanda's chair. Oscar stood at her side, looking equally outraged.

"I ain't holding her," the senator insisted. "She's free to go anytime. In fact, I wish she would."

"I'm not leaving without answers," Amanda insisted.

The senator looked to Joel and Oscar helplessly. "See what I mean? Now I think it's about time we all had a chat about this situation to see if we can't work something out."

"What *situation* is that?" Joel demanded.

"Looks as if your gal has stumbled into a hornet's nest."

Amanda took exception to the notion that she had merely *stumbled* into this story, but she kept her mouth firmly clamped shut. Joel was more than capable of telling the senator off without any help from her. And he had Oscar for backup. She shouldn't have to dig herself in any deeper for the moment.

Joel squeezed her shoulder reassuringly. "Why don't you explain just what you mean by that," he suggested.

"Well now, that's where the difficulty comes in. You see we have some issues of national security involved."

Amanda could practically hear the strains of the National Anthem underscoring his pronouncement.

From the corner, the Iraqi-maybe-CIA-operative who'd attempted to bribe her spoke up. Amazingly, his voice was unaccented now, lending some credence to Amanda's guesswork about his nationality and his profession. "Senator, I think we're going to have to bring these people into the loop."

The senator looked appalled. "We tell 'em the rest of this and it'll be all over the front page of every newspaper in the world."

"I think the operation is already compromised," the man said. "If we don't tell them, then what they do know will be printed anyway. We'd be better off giving them the whole picture and trying for damage control.''

Amanda's pulse leaped as she realized that this truly was shaping up into the biggest exposé of her career. She didn't dare reach for pencil and pad until some final decision had been reached among the key players.

Senator Rawlings considered the man's advice for several, interminable minutes, then sighed reluctantly. ''Tell 'em,'' he said. ''Maybe this once we can trust in the media's patriotism and good sense to keep silent.''

Amanda shot a look of alarm at Joel. ''Wait a minute,'' she protested. ''Joel, Oscar, are we going to agree to keep silent about what they tell us?''

Joel shook his head. ''Nobody's agreeing to anything, Amanda.'' He met her gaze evenly. ''But if they make a compelling case for national security, we have to weigh that in our decision.''

''We have a responsibility to print the truth.''

''Not at any cost. Not if lives are at stake.'' He looked toward the man whose name no one in the room had mentioned. ''Are they?''

''In a manner of speaking.''

Joel nodded slowly. ''Then I think we'd better hear the whole story.''

Amanda wanted to protest more. She wanted to leave the room and take no part in any possible cover-up, by the government or by *Inside Atlanta*. And yet her need to know the outcome, her need to understand every detail that had gone into whatever Joel's final decision would be, kept her still.

''You know already that high-tech equipment with dual private sector and military use has been shipped to Iraq,'' the man told them. ''You have linked the approval of that to Washington and, as I understand it, directly to Senator Rawlings, is that correct?''

Amanda nodded, suddenly reminded of Armand's subtle push of her subconscious in this direction. Subtle, hell. In retrospect, she realized that he'd practically spelled it out for her. It seemed she owed him for more than Henri's presence. What she'd thought of as no more than patronizing little remarks had actually been valuable clues, if she'd been smart enough to rein in her temper and listen.

''What you do not know is that the equipment is not being sold to the Iraqi government,'' the anonymous man continued.

''I don't understand,'' Amanda said.

''It is being shipped in utmost secrecy to a small group of individuals inside Iraq for what is hoped will be their eventual use in toppling the current regime.''

Amanda drew in a shaky breath as the final astonishing piece slid into place. The senator's gaze was pinned on her.

''As you can see,'' he said, ''any revelation about this will alert the Iraqi government about this covert operation. Months of laborious effort to put our people into place will be wasted. And a regime that has brutalized its own people and threatened its Arab neighbors will go on, quite possibly even stronger than before.''

He gave Amanda a stern look. ''It is in your hands, young lady.'' He glanced up at Joel. ''And yours, son. I've been where you are. I sure as hell don't envy you.''

Joel and Oscar looked shaken. Amanda's sense of ethics and responsibility warred with her ingrained belief in the public's right to know. This convoluted scheme was what Richard Howell had inadvertently stumbled into. It had gotten him murdered.

She looked at the undercover operative. "You had Richard Howell killed, didn't you?"

He looked only vaguely troubled by the accusation. Amanda was glad to see that he had some conscience left. "Well?" she prodded angrily. "Is that your answer for everything? If someone's in your way, just take them out? I suppose I should thank my lucky stars you didn't murder me and dump me by the side of some country road."

"There are always difficult choices," the man began. "We had hoped to contain this. As it turned out, you were more dogged than we had expected."

"Jesus," Amanda murmured. "I don't believe this. Our own government regards a human being as a minor inconvenience, so *pop*, he's gone."

He winced at that. In fact, everyone in the room looked damned uncomfortable. It was nothing compared to the way they'd feel when the whole truth turned up in print, she vowed.

The silence that had descended after Amanda leveled her charges went on for what seemed an eternity. It was Joel who finally broke it.

"We need to discuss this," he said, his tone somber. "I know how I feel about it, but *Inside Atlanta* is a team effort. I will not force my staff into a decision unless they are in full accord."

"I understand," the operative said. "Perhaps we could leave you alone in here to discuss it. With your permission, Senator, of course."

The senator smiled wryly. "Of course."

"It would be best," the man continued, "if none of

us left here today without a full understanding of where we stand. Far too much is at stake.''

That said, he, the senator, and Jeffrey Dunne left the room. Amanda, Oscar, and Joel exchanged silent glances.

"Okay, guys, what do you want to do?'' Joel said.

"Joel, it's your magazine, your call,'' Oscar said.

"No. I meant what I said. Amanda has busted her butt to get this story and it's a damned good one. There's a whole case to be made for the public's right to know every detail.''

"And one to be made for keeping silent,'' Amanda conceded reluctantly.

Oscar regarded her with evident surprise.

"Does that mean you're willing to wait?'' Joel asked. "Maybe hold off until this operation is played out?''

"If we do that, someone else could break the story first,'' Oscar warned. "Amanda?''

She thought of the long hours and hard work that not only she but Jenny Lee and even her mother had put in. She thought of the almost guaranteed national recognition of that work. And then she struggled with the global consequences of premature publication.

She sighed heavily, not liking the choice that had to be made or the burden of reaching that decision in such a short time. And yet, would delaying it really change the outcome? Probably not. Even so, it was the most difficult decision of her career and the one with the most far-reaching consequences.

"We wait,'' she said finally. "I don't like it, dammit, but we wait.''

Oscar shook his head. "I don't think it's quite so easy,'' he suggested.

# CHAPTER

## *Twenty-one*

A MANDA stood in front of a newsstand in Peachtree Center and admired the display of *Inside Atlanta*. She had waited five long months to get her investigation of the Iraqi undercover operation into print. Word had come from Senator Rawlings's office only hours before deadline for the latest issue that the covert mission had been a success. Oscar had immediately yanked the cover story and replaced it with her report.

Already, only hours after the edition had hit the streets, she had had congratulatory calls from around the country as word of her exposé had spread among her old journalist pals. Chad Keyes had been among the first to call.

"I'd say you clinched the Pulitzer this time," he had said. "You did a great job, Amanda."

"No hard feelings?"

"Hey, we're a competitive breed. That's the name of the game." He had paused. "I don't suppose you'd care to share any inside information you might have picked up on LeConte?"

"If I'd gotten any, I'd be glad to share it. As it turned out, he gave me a couple of nudges in the right direction, but this wasn't his game."

"Don't kid yourself, sweetheart," he warned. "If there are arms involved, LeConte's imprint is somewhere on the deal."

Amanda couldn't help thinking about that as she went back to the magazine's offices. Had she subconsciously steered away from the LeConte angle because she'd found him irresistibly charming? She hoped not. She wanted to believe that she had simply never found anything to link him directly to the operation.

Besides, she hadn't actually succumbed to all that charm. Over the past few months LeConte had called regularly, invited her to Washington, even turned up on her doorstep again, but she had managed to resist the temptation to deepen their ties beyond those of reporter and source. Since Donelli was still furious with her, it would have been all too easy to have her head turned by a man who found her intelligent, brash, and beautiful and told her so with a French accent that intoxicated like fine champagne. She figured she deserved congratulations for resisting that almost as much as she did for the investigative article that had hit the streets today.

Sighing, she pushed open the door to the *Inside Atlanta* offices and waved at the new receptionist who'd stayed on as Jenny Lee's replacement after Jenny Lee had been officially promoted to Amanda's research assistant. She was about to head into the newsroom when Oscar stepped out of his office.

"Where the devil have you been?" he grumbled. "Out admiring the new issue on the newsstands?"

"As a matter of fact, yes," she admitted.

A surprisingly boyish grin spread across his face. "Looks good, doesn't it?"

"It looks fantastic."

"So, what's next? You ain't gonna get it into your head to run out on me now that you've got your big story, are you?"

Amanda heard the note of anxiety in his voice, along with the genuine dismay of a real friend. She slowly shook her head. "No, Oscar. I'm not going to run out on you. In fact, I've been looking at houses here in Atlanta. I thought I might sell that place out in the country and move into town."

He breathed a visible sigh of relief. "So that's why there's a For Sale sign on the house."

She regarded him with astonishment. "How'd you hear about that?"

A sudden attack of coughing kept him from answering, probably because an honest reply would have necessitated his admitting that he'd been talking to Donelli. Instead, Oscar just shoved open the door to the newsroom and stood aside for her to enter.

"Surprise!"

The shouted chorus caught Amanda completely off guard. She turned to Oscar. "You old sneak," she murmured.

"Just a little party to show you you're appreciated around here. Thought maybe you needed to be reminded of that."

"Because of the For Sale sign?"

"That, too," he conceded.

Tears stung Amanda's eyes as she glanced around at the other members of the *Inside Atlanta* staff and caught sight of her parents standing in the background.

"Mom, Dad, what are you doing here?"

Her mother hugged her. "Oscar called and invited us. He said we ought to be part of the celebration, since I helped on the story. I believe he has a sentimental streak, after all."

Amanda glanced over at her boss, who was eyeing the spread of canapes with the look of a starving man. "Yes," she agreed. "I believe he does."

She studied her parents more closely. "Everything okay with you two?"

Her father and mother exchanged a look. "Better than ever," her father said.

"And, darling, guess what? I have a job," her mother announced. "One of my friends has a new art gallery in the city. I'm helping out there several days a week."

"Mother, that's wonderful." She glanced at her father. "How do you like being married to a career woman?"

"What's not to like?" he said, grinning at her mother and dropping a kiss on her cheek. He winked at Amanda. "She buys me dinner in the city once a week after work. Took me to a play last week, too. Haven't done anything like that since we first got married."

Pleased to see her parents rediscovering their love, Amanda gave them a hug and then left to circulate through the crowd. She wasn't sure she could stand there and conceal from them how much she envied their newfound happiness.

"Amanda, telephone," Jenny Lee called across the newsroom.

She grabbed the phone on the closest desk. "Hello."

"Ah, *ma chérie*, you are celebrating, I see."

"Armand," she said, unable to keep a wistful note out of her voice. Even though he could make her heart pound, it just wasn't the same as hearing the one voice she really wanted to hear, but knew she wouldn't.

"I have seen the magazine. You must be very proud."

"Thank you for helping."

"I did nothing, *ma chérie*."

"Don't be so modest," she chided. She hesitated, then asked, "Why did you help me?"

"Perhaps because I find you very beautiful."

"I'm serious."

He chuckled. "So am I, but no, you are right. That is not the whole reason. I admire initiative. I also have a deep loyalty to my friends. I wanted to be sure you would not twist their acts into something they were not. The best way to do that was to steer you toward the truth."

"Without betraying their confidence?"

"Exactly."

Amanda wasn't entirely sure whether to believe him. Still, she liked the image of Armand LeConte as a loyal friend. It pleased her to think that she had seen good in someone usually associated with evil. It was a reminder that human beings could not always be so easily labeled.

"Amanda?"

"Yes."

"You have become very quiet, *ma chérie*. Is everything all right with you?"

Everything was definitely not all right with her,

Amanda thought, but she didn't tell him that. "I'm fine, Armand."

"You sound very sad. Perhaps I should fly down and take you somewhere warm and sunny and lazy to restore your spirits."

The offer tempted far more than he could possibly imagine. "No, but thanks, anyway," she said with unmistakable regret.

"*Ma chérie*, one of these days you will say yes," he said confidently. "I can wait."

Amanda chuckled, impressed by the size of his ego. "You're outrageous, Armand."

"I know," he said, laughing with her. "*Au revoir, ma chérie.*"

"*Au revoir*," Amanda said softly, just as she looked toward the door of the newsroom and caught sight of Donelli. Her breath snagged in her throat.

He looked as if he weren't at all sure he wanted to be there. In fact, she was afraid he might bolt at any second, but then Oscar walked over and drew him in, handing him a glass of champagne and pointing him toward the hors d'oeuvres. Larry immediately joined them—the males in her life closing ranks.

Amanda sensed her parents stepping up beside her. "Darling, are you okay?" her mother asked worriedly, her gaze pinned on Donelli.

"I wish everyone would stop asking me that," Amanda snapped.

"Pumpkin," her father said, a note of censure in his voice.

Before she could respond, Donelli broke away from Oscar and Larry and started toward her. Amanda found herself suddenly oblivious to every other person in the room as she stepped forward to meet him.

"Amanda," he said, his brown eyes surveying her hungrily.

"Joe."

"Congratulations!"

"Thanks."

"I saw the sign on the house."

She nodded. "I thought I'd move into town, be a little closer to work."

"And a little farther away from me?"

"I didn't think of it that way," she said, even though it was a blatant lie. She'd wanted to escape all the memories of that house—Mack and Joe.

"Look, can we get out of here? Maybe go somewhere and talk?" he asked.

"The party's for me."

"When it's over, then?"

Amanda wasn't sure what she saw when she looked deep into his eyes. She hoped it was forgiveness. And she hoped it was mirrored in her own eyes.

"Sure," she said finally, a tiny wellspring of hope bubbling up inside her. "I'd like that."

He touched her cheek. With the pad of his thumb, he brushed away a tear she hadn't even known was there. All the time his gaze was locked with hers, making promises.

"You sure you can't get away now?" he asked, his voice husky.

Amanda glanced around, noted the fascination on every face in the room. There was bound to be speculation no matter when they left, especially if they walked out together. She shrugged finally. "Let's go."

Amusement flickered in his eyes. "Always the daredevil, huh, Amanda?"

She grinned. "Would you want me any other way?"

"No," he admitted quietly.

He held out his hand and she placed hers in it. She couldn't be absolutely certain, but she thought she heard a collective sigh of relief as they walked through the door. She knew exactly how every one of those onlookers felt. For the first time in several long, lonely months, she felt as if her world was finally righting itself.

**Watch for the next**
*Amanda Roberts*
**Mystery**

---

---

**Coming in December 1993
from Warner Books**

# CHAPTER

## *One*

THE thing Amanda Roberts liked most about her new house in the Virginia-Highlands area of Atlanta was the park a few blocks away with its stretches of grass edged by flowers and shaded by towering old trees.

The thing she hated most about her new house was its proximity to the park's jogging paths. Her friends naturally assumed she'd want to make use of those paths. Her research assistant, Jenny Lee Macon had begun coming home from work with her three nights a week just to make sure she ran—or more precisely limped—through that damned park. Amanda had tried explaining that fitness training was not part of Jenny Lee's job description, but so far her arguments had fallen on deaf ears.

On the days when she chose to be entirely honest with herself, Amanda had to admit that she felt better. Only marginally, perhaps, but better just the same. She would not have conceded that fact to Jenny Lee, however, even if she'd been taken out and tortured.

Nor, she decided as she laced up her jogging shoes, would she ever tell her that she'd actually run on her own on a night when Jenny Lee had gone off on a date with photographer Larry Carter and left Amanda to her own devices. A Tuesday, no less. An off night. Dear Lord, she hoped she wasn't becoming addicted to exercise at this late stage in her life. She popped an entire handful of jelly beans into her mouth just to prove that she hadn't entirely turned her back on sugar. She vowed to eat a huge steak tonight, too. Maybe a hot fudge sundae.

When Amanda reached the park, the paths were teeming with runners, bikers, and folks out for a brisk walk on the chilly spring night. She spent a dutiful ten minutes doing her stretching exercises, then set off at a clip that wouldn't exactly be a threat to an Olympic competitor. She smiled and waved to half a dozen people she recognized from other nights.

There was something comforting about feeling that she was already a part of her new neighborhood.

As she ran, her mind miraculously cleared, quite possibly because she couldn't concentrate on anything except catching her breath. When she'd completed the mile-long route she and Jenny Lee usually covered, she felt so good she decided to push for one more mile.

Her legs began to feel like lead after the first quarter-mile. Then she got a stitch in her side that hobbled her. With her breath coming in ragged gasps, she stopped beside the path and bent over, trying to catch her breath.

"Are you okay?" a softly accented voice asked with concern.

Amanda looked up at the woman who'd stopped to check on her. With a thin, athletic build, eyes the color of a vivid blue sky and skin that had been turned a tawny gold by the sun, she looked vibrantly healthy. Her hair, long and professionally highlighted, was caught up in a ponytail, a severe style that would have been devastating on anyone whose features weren't as perfect as this woman's. She looked to be in her late twenties, thirty at the outside.

"More or less," Amanda told her, with a wry grimace. "I tried to push myself."

The woman smiled sympathetically, still jogging in

place. "I could wait and run with you, just to be sure you make it back okay."

"No, really. Thanks, but I'd just slow you down. You look as if you train for marathons."

"As a matter of fact, I do. It relieves the stress. It also allows me to eat anything I want to," she admitted with a rueful expression. "I'd hate to give up cheesecake."

Amanda couldn't recall the last time she had allowed herself to indulge in cheesecake. "Exactly how far do you have to run to do that?" she inquired somewhat wistfully.

"I aim for six to ten miles at least three or four times a week."

Amanda groaned. "I guess I'll stick to no-fat frozen yogurt."

The other woman laughed. "You sure you don't want me to wait for you?"

"No, really. I'll be fine," she said. "The pain in my side is going and I can almost breathe normally again."

"See you then. Take it easy."

" 'Bye." Envious, Amanda watched her move off, her long stride looking effortless. She actually tried to mimic it for another hundred yards before conceding that she'd had it for the night. Besides, the sun was rapidly sinking and she had no desire to be stranded on the far side of the park after nightfall. The lighting wasn't all that terrific. The city had probably skimped on mercury vapor lights just to plant all those flowers.

Amanda took a shortcut back to her starting point, then walked slowly back home, relieved when she was finally inside, showered, and ready to eat the huge salad she'd brought home from the grocery store. She promised herself she'd have that steak tomorrow night.

Just after eleven, when she'd settled in bed with a book she'd been trying for the last month to find time to read, the phone rang.

"Amanda, honey, is that you?" Jenny Lee asked worriedly.

"Who else were you expecting? You called my number."

"Were you watching the news?"

"No, why?" she said, instantly alerted by Jenny Lee's tone.

"Another woman's missing," she said. "She disappeared tonight and right from that park by your house. I was so worried that you might have been over there."

"Actually, I was," Amanda said, her adrenaline pumping.

Five women had disappeared over the last year and a half. Six, now. All of them had been young. All professionals. All beautiful. Beyond that, however, the police had not discovered a single link. While each was officially considered a separate homicide, unofficially the search for a common thread continued. Women all over the city were panicking, especially since the latest disappearances had come only weeks apart, suggesting that if a serial killer was in fact involved, he was becoming bolder and more desperate.

"What did they say on the news?"

"Not much. A friend reported her missing when she didn't come home from her run, but the police won't release an ID until they notify her family. It gave me the creeps listening to them, though. Do you think this is related to all those others?"

"It's possible."

"Amanda, do you think maybe we ought to investigate this for *Inside Atlanta*. Maybe profile these women or something?"

"I was just thinking the same thing. Let's talk to Oscar about it in the morning."

"Okay. Good night, Amanda. Be careful."

"I'm always careful, Jenny Lee." Even though she knew that was true, Amanda immediately got out of bed and walked from room to room, checking the locks on the windows and doors. Back in her bedroom, she even searched the closet until she found the gun she'd had ever since an unhappy subject of one of her exposés in New York had targeted her for bomb threats and other misfortunes. So far, she'd never had to use it. She prayed almost daily that she never would. Still, she felt better once it was tucked away in her bedside nightstand.

Not five minutes later the phone rang again.

"Amanda?" Donelli's voice sounded almost as anxious as Jenny Lee's. It was also tinged with an awareness that despite the recent improvement in their relationship, he still had no official claims on her, including no right to openly worry about her.

"Hi. Yes, I know about the disappearance. Yes, I was in the park tonight. Yes, I'm fine."

"Okay. Okay. You can't blame a guy for worrying."

"No, I suppose not. How are you? Did you get the fields planted today?" she asked, even though it killed her to feign an interest in Donelli's farming, when she thought he ought to be doing private investigations like the detective he had once been.

"Corn's in. The tomatoes will be in tomorrow. I'll probably do the beans the day after."

He sounded so damned pleased, she wanted to drive out to the country and shake him. "Joe, do you think this disappearance is related to the others?"

"The cops don't even know if the first five are linked."

"Maybe not officially, but what does your gut instinct tell you?"

"They're linked."

"I was thinking of looking into this, maybe profiling the women."

"Why doesn't that surprise me?"

She waited for his objection. "No lectures?"

"Not from me. I learned long ago I can't stop you from doing something once you've set your mind on it."

She sighed and hugged the phone a little tighter. "Thank you."

"I'll talk to you in the morning, okay?"

"Okay. Night, Joe."

"Good night, darlin'."

Smiling at the hint of Southern dialect mellowing his native Brooklyn accent, Amanda hung up and drifted to sleep.

First thing in the morning, eager to get to work and map out a plan with Jenny Lee and Oscar, she grabbed the paper and took off for the *Inside Atlanta* offices. Only when she was at her desk, coffee cup in hand, did she spread open the *Constitution*.

A sense of horror and unreality slammed through her as she stared at the front page. MISSING WOMAN DISAPPEARS ON RUN declared the four-column headline. But that was no surprise. What made Amanda's stomach pitch acid and sent a cold chill down her spine was the picture that went with the story. Although black and white and smudged, there was no mistaking that gorgeous, delicate face, that mane of golden streaked hair.

Lynette Rogers. Twenty-eight. A stockbroker. A marathon runner.

And the woman who'd taken time out to offer assistance to Amanda, perhaps only minutes before she had vanished.

# By the year 2000, 2 out of 3 Americans could be illiterate.

It's true.

Today, 75 million adults… about one American in three, can't read adequately. And by the year 2000, U.S. News & World Report envisions an America with a literacy rate of only 30%.

Before that America comes to be, you can stop it… by joining the fight against illiteracy today.

Call the Coalition for Literacy at toll-free **1-800-228-8813** and volunteer.

## Volunteer Against Illiteracy. The only degree you need is a degree of caring.

Ad Council Coalition for Literacy